All About Mary

A Mick Hart Mystery

By Lawrence Christopher

Also by Lawrence Christopher

Dog 'Em: A Mick Hart Mystery (The Novella)

Visit TimBookTu.com for short story fictions by Lawrence Christopher

Published by MF Unlimited
Civic Center Station
P. O. Box 55346
Atlanta, GA 30308
MFUnltd@aol.com

Book cover design by The Ly Group, Tolbert Graphics and LCAA

Dedication

Hallelujah! I give you the highest praise.

O give thanks unto the Lord, for He is good: for His mercy

endureth for ever. Psalms 107: 1

Acknowledgements

To my teachers at Robert T. Fulton Elementary and Jesup W. Scott High schools, "a, b, c, d, e, f, g, h, I, j, k, l, m, n, o, p, q, r, s, t, u, v, w, x, y and z, a, e, I, o, u and sometimes y." I remembered. Without you teaching me to put these in the correct order, this novella obviously would not have been possible. To all teachers, I thank you with much love and appreciation.

Thanks to everyone who logged online to TimBookTu.com and followed the "Kickin' It with Mary" series and wanted more. Thanks to Mr. Memphis Vaughn, Editor of TimBookTu.com, for your support by publishing me on your award winning prestigious site and for choosing me as a 'Featured Writer of the Month.'

I dedicate "Kickin' It With Mary Again" to Ms. Sonya Senell Wash, author of *R.I.P. Till We Meet Again*, ARA Publishing. Thank you Sonya for wanting to know more. To Pashonia S. Robinson author of *Bad By Myself*, Black Ink Publishing Co., you said it was easy. To both of you, I thank you for your guidance and inspiration.

Special thanks to Ms. Carolyn Lindsey short story author and playwright on TimBookTu.com. Your support has gained you appointment as President of the Lawrence Christopher Fan Club. ☺ And special thanks to Mr. Tony Lindsay, author of "One Dead Preacher" Black Words, Inc.

Thank you Editors Ms. Patricia Brooks Ly and Ms. Vivian E. Driver and Angie Buck.

Much appreciation to Williams July, II, author of books *Brothers, Lust and Love* and *Understanding the Tin Man*, Doubleday. Without your direction, encouragement and guidance, this project might have never come to fruition. Thank you my Moabite brother.

Kudos for "Kickin' It with Mary"

I really enjoyed this story of yours. It captured my attention and the   Carolyn
*reality was heart felt. Thank you, for taking your many other readers
and me into your created world of written expression. I look forward
to reading more of your works, posted on the TimBookTu.com site.
Hey... Keep The Creativity Flowing!*

I just read "Kickin It with Mary". To say that I read it from   Jhori
*beginning to end...non stop...running over periods and everything...is
an understatement. Very well done Mr. Christopher. Like I said, I
think everyone knows a "Mary" and even some of us have a little of
her inside of us. So used to being abused and dogged that you don't
know how to accept being treated well. Funny how you can accept
the bad far better than the good.*

I loved "Kickin' it with Mary" and the sequel! It was excellent, even   Karen
*made me a little teary-eyed. I wish you much success in your future
endeavors. Well, I've got to get back to work. I'll definitely check
out your other works later.*

Great Story! I've enjoyed reading the "Kickin' it with Mary" series.   Kim
*This would have been a great novel...you really don't see too many
stories from a man's point of view, especially trying to change a
woman whose life has been through so many tribulations as Mary's.
Thanks for giving the audience good stories to read.*

I have just finished reading "Kickin it with Mary," and "Kickin it   Michelle
*with Mary Again", please tell me that these are just two chapters
from a book that you are selling out the back of your car!*

After reading "Kicking It With Mary" I almost cried. It was so   Romona
*touching. While reading it, Mary became my friend whom I wanted
to reach out and help and at times she even became part of the old
me. Oh to have a real Prince Charming like that.*

That story about Mary was so beautiful. The less than perfect sistas   Stephanie
*out there are neglected when it comes to quality fiction. Thank you
for showing the beauty in our imperfection.*

Table of Contents

Introduction

Love . . .

. . . bears all things,
believes all things,
hopes all things,

Love never fails.

1Corinthians 13: 7-8

Prologue

Mary Jane

"I'm in love with Mary Jane
She's my main thang
She makes me feel all right
She makes my heart sang
And when I'm feeling low
She comes as no surprise
Turns me on with her love
Takes me to paradise . . .

"I'm in love with Mary Jane
I'm not the only one
Mary want's to play around
I let her have her fun
She's not the kind of girl
That you can just tie down
She likes to spread her love
And turn your head around . . ."

Rick James; <u>Come Get It</u> (1978)

I.   Bloody Mary (Mick)

It is an open and shut case as far as the Odelot Homicide Detectives are concerned. Perry Rogers, 32 was arrested and charged with the murder of Mary Jane Jenkins, a 25 years old single mother of two. The murder victim was also Perry Rogers' live-in fiancée. It was Perry who called 911 to report the murder. When the police arrived at his house, they found Perry with Mary's multiple stabbed body and the suspected murder weapon kitchen knife with his prints on it. Mary's two children, Sapphire age seven and Gerald age six were in the house while the police questioned and took Perry into custody.   An undisclosed family member was noted in the police report as having temporary custody of the children. That was as much as I could get over the phone from my long time friend and homicide detective McIntosh.

Perry Rogers' mother called the office, Mick Hart Investigations, asking me to look into the arrest of her son. I told Mrs. Rogers over the phone that I didn't see anything that I could do to aid in her son's case. But the devoted mother was insistent. So, I agreed to meet her for an initial consultation.

"My son did not kill that girl, Mr. Hart," testified Mrs. Rogers.

"I'm afraid evidence would prove otherwise Mrs. Rogers. The police have a pretty tight case against your son. His fingerprints are on the knife that stabbed his fiancée, . . . Mary Jane Jenkins," I reminded the mother.

"That don't mean a thing. Police always have tight cases against innocent black men, till somebody prove them wrong."

"Mrs. Rogers, your son isn't helping himself by not talking to the police. If he didn't do it and knows who did, then it would make sense that he would tell the police."

"Sometimes it's best if you keep quiet and let the Lord do all the talking for you."

"I'm not much of a religious man, Mrs. Rogers. But I know that if you believed that, you wouldn't be talking to me right now. The truth of the matter is, God might be the only one who can save your son."

Okay, maybe this is one of those cases of God working in mysterious ways. How many times has a murder mystery begun with an innocent person being wrongly accused of the crime? How many times has some bumbling detective or clever sleuth come along to save the innocent from being wrongly convicted and catching the real murderer? The answer is, way too many times. Call it God working in mysterious ways or whatever you like. It happens. I only pray that it would happen in this case, because I told Mrs. Rogers that I would look into it.

I promised Mrs. Rogers seventy-two hours at no charge. My caseloads of tracking down deadbeat child supporters and missing persons are kind of light. A face to face conversation with Detective McIntosh of the Odelot Police Department and Perry Rogers will probably be all that's necessary to bring this case to a close.

Benjamin McIntosh and I are former high school buddies. We played on the football team. I was the quarterback and Mac was the center. After four years of trying, our senior year, we brought home the Ohio State championship trophy in AAA football. Four years of me barking out signal plays for the Bulldogs to execute is a distant memory, but that camaraderie it spawned remains. Mac is more in charge now, being the lead detective in the homicide unit of the OPD. He gives the orders and doesn't like it when our cases overlap.

I'm a private investigator, not by choice but for needed income. I was fired from my job as a debt collector, for tracking down the father of the child of a teenage single mother. The teenage mother was being sought for a delinquent gas bill and had little means of paying. When she told me of her situation, I queried about someone who could help her, namely, the father of her child for one. She told me she didn't know where he was. It was my job as a bill collector to find what we called "skips." Inappropriately mind you, I found the father. He was married and had a well paying job. I made a few phone calls and got the man to make financial restitution. A few months later, I was called into a meeting where one of the collection agency's largest clients allegedly received complaints about our collection tactics. I was the lead collector at the time and was rightly blamed. On the recommendation and hook-up of a former coworker, now partner in the agency, I began finding deadbeat parents and missing persons for a living.

There are two kinds of missing persons; those lost and those hiding. In the case of Perry Rogers, if there were such a missing person to be found, it would be the latter. If as his mother believes, that Perry did not kill Mary Jane Jenkins, then there was a killer who had to be found.

My investigation starts at the office of Detective Benjamin McIntosh. Mac's reception of me would be determined on his caseload and how many of his open cases were solvable. One thing I had on my side in this case was that as far as the OPD was concerned, this was an open and shut case. Unfortunately, that is the same thing that may work against me. If Mac feels that I'm going to cause trouble by meddling in a closed case, then his reception may be unresponsive. Here goes nothing.

"Big Mac, what's shaking?" I express as I walk into his office. The big man is sitting behind a cluttered desk. Luck is on my side. He's smiling.

"Mick! Here man, read this? Someone sent this to me in an email." He hands me a sheet of paper.

A Walk in the Woods

An atheist was taking a walk through the woods, admiring all that the 'accident of evolution' had created. "What majestic trees! What powerful rivers! What beautiful animals!" he said to himself.

As he walked alongside the river he heard a rustling in the bushes behind him. As he turned to look, he saw a 7-foot grizzly charge towards him. He ran as fast as he could up the path. He looked over his shoulder & saw the bear closing in on him. He tried to run even faster, so scared that tears were coming to his eyes. He looked over his shoulder again, and the bear was even closer.

His heart was pumping frantically as he tried to run even faster, but he tripped and fell on the ground. He rolled over to pick himself up and saw the bear right on top of him raising his paw to kill him. At that instant he cried out "Oh my God!"

Just then, time stopped.

The bear froze; the forest was silent; the river even stopped moving. A bright light shone upon the man, and a voice came out of the sky saying...

"You deny my existence all of these years; teach others I don't exist; even credit my creation to a cosmic accident, and now do you expect me to help you out of this predicament?

"Am I to count you as a believer?"

The atheist, ever so proud, looked into the light and said...

"It would be rather hypocritical to ask to be a Christian after all these years, but could you make the bear a Christian?"

"Very well," said the voice.

As the light went out, the river ran, and the sounds of the forest continued, the bear put his paw down. The bear then brought both paws together bowed his head and said...

"Lord, I thank you for this food, which I am about to receive."

The funniest thing about the joke is that I had heard it told from the pulpit by my pastor Reverend Doctor I. M. Lowdown a few Sundays past. There is one thing that can be said about electronic mailing. You can always find a good joke being passed around at the click of a button. A good email joke can make its way around the globe in a matter of minutes, while my telephone bill dropped in a mailbox can't make it across town in two days. I laugh at the joke as if it were new to me. Mac's eyes are still teary from his jovial reaction to the story. It's a good time to hit him up for information.

"To what do I owe this visit from the great PI, Mick Hart?" Mac asks.

"I don't know who that would be, but this Mick Hart needs a little information."

"For you my friend, anything. Shoot."

"It's about the Rogers case. Perry Rogers." The smile and lightheartedness seem to fade from Mac's face. I didn't let that stop me. "His mother seems to think he didn't kill this, Mary Jane Jenkins. I told her it was a hopeless cause, but that I would look into it for her."

"You're smart to tell her that. I hope you didn't take any of the poor woman's money. The only thing we don't have on Mr. Rogers is a confession. Otherwise, it's a done deal."

"Don't you think that's odd. Why wouldn't he confess with all that you have against him?"

"Look Mick, don't waste your time with this one. We have the weapon, with his prints on it. We have motive, his fiancée was cheating on him. Evidence indicates it was a crime of passion. DNA testing shows she had sex with someone other than the *perp* the night she was killed."

"But you don't have a confession yet." I remind Mac.

"Don't mess with this case Mick."

"I promised his mother three days worth of investigations, that's all. After that, I'm done. May I see the case file?" Mac gives me a leering glance before handing over a manila folder retrieved from a file drawer.

"I don't mind showing you this, because there is nothing in there that is going to help your investigation. The man came home found his fiancée getting *boinked* by another man and he killed her."

"What about this other man, do we have any evidence of him other than the semen? Any witnesses?"

"No, the only one else in the house was the kids. This Mary Jane Jenkins had two kids from prior relationships. The officer on the scene finds Rogers next to the body."

"And he makes no attempt to hide anything?"
"None. I wish all my cases were this easy."

In the front of the folder are photos of the crime scene. Mary Jane Jenkins; it is the first time I see her. She is pretty, even blood stained. Mary's complexion is a French Vanilla Cappuccino and the color of her hair including her eyebrows, is that of the froth. It took me a moment to take my eyes away from her face. If she looks this appealing dead, I can imagine her beauty with her face full of life. I didn't know Mary Jane Jenkins and no one has told me anything about her. There is no testimony for me to believe anyone's story about the murder. As far as I know and see, Mary Jane Jenkins, as beautiful as she is, didn't deserve to die.

~~~~~~~

Luck is on my side. The first patrolman on the scene, responding to the 911 call is *in the house*... that would be the squad room. I catch him just before he's about to go on his shift. He's a young black cop, who I haven't seen before. That's good, because he won't be biased talking to a PI looking for information.

"Officer Wash, I'm Mick Hart." I extend my hand for an introductory shake.
"Hey."
"I just left Detective McIntosh's office, going over the murder case you handled last week." I used Mac's name to give me some credibility.
"Yeah."
"I was wondering if you can give me some details about the case."
"What, you a reporter or something?"
"No. I'm a private investigator."
"I filed a thorough report."
"Yes you did. I'm just a face-to-face kind of guy. Reading facts off a report only does so much for me. So you got a minute?"
"Sure."
"Who let you in the house?"

"The little boy. The *perp* was upstairs with the body. The little girl was standing next him. Strange too."

"What do you mean?"

"I mean the little girl was standing there looking at her mother lying in the bed dead and she wasn't crying or anything."

"What about Rogers?"

"He was the one doing all the crying. You know, hard like, body shaking crying."

"And he was holding the knife that was used on the Jenkins woman?"

"Yeah. I had to draw my piece to get him to drop it."

"He said nothing to you?"

"Nope."

"Was there anything about the scene that stood out?"

"Not really. Everything is documented in my report. Somebody was having a party up in that bedroom. The windows were wide open. But you could still smell what was going on. There was an empty pint of E&J. Tobacco was in an ashtray by the bed. They gutted some cigars to smoke marijuana in the skin."

"How was the body?"

"That was weird too. She was covered up. Maybe he did it because of the little girl."

~~~~~~~

After speaking with Officer Wash, I stopped by the city morgue to talk to the medical examiner, Susan. Susan and I have a long-standing working relationship. The morgue is my first stop in a *lost*, missing person case. If I don't find who I'm looking for there, it is a good start.

"Hey Susan."

"Mick. Long time, no see."

"In my case, that's a good thing. That means I'm not looking for someone who might be dead."

"Is that all our relationship is Mick? I let you come down here and get off on some freaky fetish by looking at naked corpses."

"No. I also like your cold hands."

"Yeah right. Who are you looking for now, another Jane Doe?"

"Actually, I wanted to talk about a Mary Jane Jenkins."
"What a surprise, you have a name this time. Jenkins, ah yeah. Broken cervix, multiple stab wounds."
"What killed her?"
"Hmmm. The official cause of death is asphyxiation. The bruises on her neck are consistent with strangulation from a strong right hand."
"What about the stab wounds?"
"The doer must have been real crazed. She was stabbed nine times, but only one might have been fatal."
"Might?"
"Yeah. There was one puncture to the heart, but it occurred after she was dead. The other punctures weren't deep enough to cause any fatal damage. It was like he was just angry and was stabbing out of rage."
"Mac said she had sex right before she was killed."
"Yeah. There was seminal discharge in the vaginal area."
"Any signs of force?"
"There were some bruising, consistent with rape, but it could have been recreational and a rough go at it. This girl would bruise easily."

"So she could have been raped?"
"Possible. She also had a high blood alcohol content and there was a trace of marijuana in her system. This girl was partying the night she was killed. Pretty girl too."
"Yes, I know. I saw the photos from the crime scene."
"Not that I want to contribute to your sick fetish, but her body is still here if you want to take a look. No one has claimed it yet. I did the autopsy a couple of days ago."

It had been a week since Mary Jane Jenkins died. No one yet claimed the body for burial. What about Mary's family? Susan pulled out the drawer that contained the lifeless body of Mary Jane Jenkins. The photos didn't do her justice. Mary was far more attractive in person. Her full-lips were naturally pouting. Sandy hair complimented her light complexion. She wasn't a small runway model woman. She was full-figured and shapely. She had those nice big upper 'mother's arms.' I could see Mary wearing a bright colored sundress and having all men in sight revolving around her just to bask in her presence.

But now Mary's light had been snuffed out. Mac's hold on to the motive of a jealous man seeking revenge' had more bearing now that I was face to lifeless face with Mary. She still appeared desirable to me. So if that is all there was to it, then why no confession. It is now time to talk to Perry Rogers, the suspected murderer, and the jilted fiancé to hear his side of the story.

II.   Kickin' It with Mary (Perry)

*K*ickin' it is what they call it today. In the old school days, it was called a *relationship*, for better or worse. A relationship between a man and woman, involves the dating, the support and affection shared there of. *Kickin' it* means, I'm in it for me.

The first time I saw Mary was in a Burger King restaurant. She was a voluptuous, short woman with curves on her body to be seen from every angle. She was a thick sistah who was probably a cheeseburger away from 200 pounds. Her face was as pretty as any other, with penetrating eyes, and a hypnotic smile. There was without a doubt a physical attraction.

I was two places in line behind Mary and her two children. Her children; a boy and a girl looked to be about five and six years of age. An older man draped in gold chains, with matching rings was next in line behind Mary, and I watched him eyeing her and trying to make small talk. He complimented her on her cute children. When it was Mary's turn to order, the children offered up what they wanted. "I want the one with the toy mommy." "Me too," they blurted. Just as quickly, Mary responded with "No. I told you I don't have no money for that." That was all she needed to say and Mr. Goldie pulled out a money clip and shuffled through a selection of currency to cover the order. Mary looked from his fist full of dollars to his face and said "thank you" with a smile that made every man in line extremely jealous.

I left the newly found couple and family sitting at a table eating and talking. I was glad to have left the fast food chain that night, because from the moment I saw Mary, I had coveted and lusted after her. Only later to become envious of the man who had won her as his prize for the moment. It was all behind me now . . . so I thought.

Two weeks later on a hot summer day, I was driving and spotted Mary and her children walking. Mary was actually hobbling with a bandage around her left knee. I would like to say it was the Good

Samaritan in me, but I have to admit that the sight of her big thick thighs in a pair of shorts greatly influenced my decision to offer them a ride. I drove the family to a medical clinic where Mary was having her injured knee from a car accident checked out. Mary's car had been totaled in the accident.

After leaving them at the clinic's door, Mary thanked me, then ordered her children to thank me. Half way down the street, I found myself turning around, parking in the clinic's lot and waiting. About an hour and a half later, out comes Mary and the kids. The boy was crying, whining about having to walk. That is when I pulled up. "May I offer you a lift?" I asked. It took less than a moment for Mary to accept my invitation. The little boy, Gerald, must have seen me as a gift horse. Once settled in the backseat, he asked for some ice cream, with his sister, Sapphire, seconding his request. Mary said nothing. She did look at me with those penetrating eyes of hers, which looked in my head and without saying a word I knew she wanted some ice cream as well. The next thing I knew, I was offering and there we were in Baskin Robbins 31 Flavors enjoying four of their offerings.

I spent time getting to know Mary, the person behind the beauty and the body. She was 25 years of age, raising her two kids, living in low income housing, on the salary of a Tele-marketer. There were six years between our ages. The only information I cared about was whether there was a man in her life. She said no one special. Mary gave me her beeper number and instructed me to *hit her on the hip* some time. I know that should have been my first clue. A woman who gives her beeper number instead of her home phone number should be suspect.

I waited a week before I paged Mary. The following day was when she returned the call. I offered to take her out to dinner and to the movies. Mary accepted and we went out for the first time. The children were with her sister. The night's events were pleasant and the pleasantries continued at my house. We had several glasses of wine and talked late into the night.

Mary's life story was that of struggle and growing up in the streets. Her mother put her and her sister out at an early age, over the man their mother was shacking with. The man approached Mary and her older sister for sex and when they told their mother, she didn't believe them. The girls went to live with an aunt who was on welfare, and supplemented her income with prostitution. Knowing the environment

Mary came from helped me understand Mary's idea of the man\woman relationship. It was about bartering to her. There was no bonding or carryover of the relationship passed the current exchange of favors. Mary spent the night at my house and we had unbridled sex. Her body was truly like butter, soft and smooth to the touch and when it became hot, it was easy to spread. My fingers would sink deeply in the folds and mounds of Mary's flesh. Despite the rotund size of Mary's legs, she was surprisingly limber. Her thick thighs pushing against one another kneaded them into a fluffy passageway. It was indeed my pleasure in viewing her jiggle and wiggle as she moved about my king-size bed. Mary's agility inspired the best sex I've had with any woman.

When morning came, I awoke in the gaze of a beautiful face sleeping in front of me, eye bugger included. I draped the back of my hand across Mary's bare arm to verify the smoothness I felt in the night. It was real and so was she. I had not dreamt it. My body was relaxed and so was my mind. I mistook my physical satisfaction for a sense of emotional joy and called it love. When Mary woke, she did not say much. She grabbed her purse, pulled out a toothbrush and washcloth and told me she had to pick up her children.

After that night I paged Mary for a week, *blowing her pager up*, with no return call. What should have been chalked up as the best one nightstand ever for me, was erased when I received a call from Mary. She asked me if I would give her a ride to pick up her children. Without hesitation, I replied "yes." Whatever Mary wants, Mary gets. Returning Mary and her children to her apartment, I asked if I could come in. She hesitated for a moment, but conceded.

The living room was a mess with evidence of a party. Wine glasses and beer bottles were about the tables and residue of incense and marijuana was in the air. Mary began picking up around the apartment. I could only imagine what had gone on and it made me resentful that I wasn't a part of it. I didn't know how to broach the subject other than to ask directly why she hadn't return my pages. "I've been busy," was her aloof reply. Busy doing what is what I didn't want to know. Mary went about the chore of cleaning the apartment as if I weren't there. When she pulled out the vacuum I took that as my queue to leave. There was no attempt to stop me. On my way home, I vowed never to call Mary again.

It wasn't as hard as I thought to put Mary out of my mind after gaining control of my hormones. That was until one Friday night, late.

Mary calls out of the midnight blue and asks, "what I'm doing" as if we were old friends checking in on one another. It had been a long day at work so I convey enough to tell her that. I doubt that she heard a word I said. As soon as I came to a notable pause Mary asks me if I want to come over and she gave me her preference for some wine. My hormones sprung into action and stood up in my pants.

A stop at a corner store on my way to Mary's, I bought a couple of bottles of Spumante. Mary could put away some alcohol. I showed up about 12:15 a.m. and Mary came to the door wearing nothing but a man's under-shirt and thong panties. The sleeveless type. Her breasts were swinging, as were her hips as she walked. Thick, meaty and sheeny legs were the most incredible sights I had ever seen. Mary sat on the couch pulling her heavy, hairless legs beneath her big bottom. The kids were asleep in their room.

On the table were two wineglasses. We began drinking and talking. With more drinking came more talking. I knew where the night was headed and I was going along for the ride and the ride to come. Before the inevitable sex drive, there came a bump in the road. I'm not sure if it was the Spumante or the *joint* Mary lit, but she became very comfortable with disclosing more of her life story. She did say that she was surprised that I was still calling her. She said that most guys don't call again after they get in her pants. If they do call again, it's for a second helping only. I guess that made me special or just like the rest.

The story of her life sounded made up, until I saw watery eyes at points of painful memories. But tears can be manufactured. Nonetheless, the story was painful to hear and heartbreaking. Everything from a drunkard father, to an abusive mother to men coming and going, including her children's father. Men abused her, misused and used her. She told me of personal and professional tragedies of rape episodes and being caught up in the legal and welfare system. I sat dumbfounded by what I heard. To keep from being pulled totally in by what could be an award winning performance, I listened with a skeptic ear. Mary told some parts of the story convincingly and nonchalantly, as if she had placed the hurt behind her. I came to believe her. During the course of the late night, Mary's phone rang and her pager beeped several times. She ignored them. I suspected they were *booty calls* gone unanswered.

A quiet moment fell and Mary moved on. She stretched out one of her pillowy legs and placed her foot against my thigh. She gazed at me with lazy eyes, giving me a look that every man knows when he sees it and sometimes can't believe it. There was no more talking. Mary stood from the couch and reached out her hand for mine. She led me to the bedroom where she showed me a *sexplosive* night. That's why my *boy* gave her a return standing ovation for each performance. With that aside, the best part of that night was going to sleep holding Mary in my arms. I have had sex with many women and afterwards fallen asleep on the far side of the bed. But there was something about holding Mary.

Saturday morning came bright and early. Once again I looked into the face of a sleeping beauty. Thoughts of the night came flooding into my head. An instant hard-on erected. Instead of acting on the impulsive urge, I climbed out of bed headed for the kitchen, when one of life's awkward moments occurred. Sapphire sat outside her mother's door, holding open a half-gallon of milk. "Is this any good? I'm hungry," she stated. I felt as if I needed to explain why I was coming out of her mother's room this early in the morning. Sadly, the little girl didn't need any explanation. I probably wasn't the first and I wouldn't be the last. I looked at the expiration date on the carton and gave the contents a whiff. "It's good." I assured her.

I followed the little girl to the kitchen to quench my parched mouth. Gerald, Mary's son sat on the floor watching cartoons. He paused for a moment to see who the overnight guest was this time. There was no reaction on his face. He turned back to his television viewing. "My brother, he don't eat breakfast," Sapphire offered. The little girl opened the refrigerator to retrieve a box of cereal. Inside the refrigerator were an assortment of bags and Styrofoam containers from fast food and take out restaurants.

I sat in the kitchen getting to know Sapphire, who was a bright little girl for six. She confirmed her age to me before she told me about her dream. Once she paused which I never thought she would, I went and sat with Gerald in the living room. He was just the opposite of his sister. He had very little to say even upon my asking. I concluded that they were good kids with potential. I felt the same about their mother, convincing myself that what they needed was a stable home environment and a good man to take care of them. I went to Mary's bedroom to propose to be that man.

Mary stirred and moaned with pleasure when I wrapped my arms around her and squeezed one of her fleshy breasts. She backed herself into me, laying one of her soft legs across me. We did the simulated bump and grind for as long as we could until the real event had to take place. Once that love making session was over Mary left the room. While she was gone, I decided to suggest that she and I hookup for the long term. I knew it was crazy to even think, but I liked Mary and her kids. I knew that given the right opportunity and support, their lives would be different. I was prepared to make that commitment to be that support, and to make that difference.

Mary returned to the bedroom with a request perched on her lips, "I need a favor." Immediately, I thought to myself, "what did last night cost me?" Was Mary's service just a prelude to returning a *favor* upon request? The answer was sure to follow. "I need a hundred fifty dollars," Mary voiced. It wasn't as much of a shock to me as it could have been. I knew Mary better now and how she operated. I was one of probably many men with whom she swapped favors. In order for me to make a difference in Mary's life I had to start right then and there.

"You know you could have just asked me," I informed her.

"What are you talking about?" Mary replied.

"You could have just asked me for the money. You didn't have to do what you did last night and this morning to get it... Not that I'm complaining."

"What are you trying to say?"

"I'm saying that as a friend, I would have given you the money if only you had asked."

"Oh really." Mary sounded disbelieving. "No questions asked?"

"I wouldn't say all that. I would want to know if this was a loan or a gift."

"You wouldn't want to know why I needed the money?"

"Not necessarily. Should I?"

There was a long pause after that question. Mary looked around the room seemingly trying to avoid looking directly at me. Then she let out a long exhausting sigh, followed by a slow stream of tears. I wondered if another great performance was about to follow. Then she let it out.

"I need the money to pay for an abortion." Mary divulged. Now she looked right at me, to note my reaction no doubt. I didn't let the brain churn be noted on my face. Knowing that we had practiced safe sex, for the most part anyway, I was assured the unborn wasn't mine. But did that matter? I had just convinced myself to be supportive of this woman, however this was not part of the equation. Being supportive would mean the killing of a child. By saying no, it could mean a child would be born in an already messed up situation or Mary would find another friend to give her the money. Mary's eyes remained on me and asked, "So what?"

"What do you mean, so what?" I replied.
"Can you lend me the money or what?"
"Of course I can. But what about asking the father?"
"He said it wasn't his and I didn't want to argue with his no good ass."
"Instead, you would ask someone else."
"If you don't want to give me the money then just say so. I don't need to hear a bunch of shit."
"You're right, you don't need to hear a bunch of shit. What you need to hear is that you need to change your life around and stop sleeping with men who only care to go to bed with you. They may buy you material things, take you out to eat or pay some of your bills. There is more to a relationship than that. Or at least there should be. Maybe not for them, but it should be for you. You have two children in there. They need . . ."
Cutting me off, Mary wailed out, "What? What do they need? Some sorry ass man to lie to them, make broken promises, try to be a daddy when he's around then leave when he's tired of the responsibility. I don't think so. I can do bad by myself."
"And that you seem to be doing, bad, by yourself."
"Are you going to give me the money or what?"

My head was reeling between yes, no, yes, no. I wanted to reach across the bed and shake the decision out of my head and some sense into Mary. Yes is what I decided on, I would give her the money and I would never call Mary again. I saw the potential of what she could be, but in order for Mary to be better than she was, she had to see the potential within herself.

I had to drive to an ATM to get the money. Mary didn't have a checking account, so she would have been charged for cashing the check at some corner store or check cashing company. It was a long drive for me. I didn't feel good at all about what I was contributing to. Losing the relationship with Mary and her children also hurt me. When I handed Mary the money, she hugged me and kissed me. There was no feeling in my kiss. There was no feeling in me. I was finished.

A week later I got a call from Mary, a message left on my answering machine. Okay, so I went.

III.   Oh Mary Don't You Weep (Mick)

See no evil. Hear no evil. Speak no Evil.

Perry is a man who has been *hopelessly in love and out of control.* Mary had opened Perry's nose, and he got a big whiff of her sex. Now he's got the *Fever*, as sung by Lalah Hathaway accompanied by Joe Sample. I don't see the relationship as being anything more than one based on the satisfaction of either parties' desires, *kickin' it.* Mary needed or wanted money or a good time. Perry wanted someone to fulfill his wanton lust. They both got what they deserved. Well, except Mary. She didn't deserve to die.

After listening to Perry Rogers' first account of his encounter with Mary, I decide to find out what I can about the woman in question. There is no question that Mary is dead. The question is who killed her, and why. To find out about Mary, why not go to the source, to the woman who brought her into the world.

I arrive at 1617 Foster Street, to a seemingly rundown house in the middle of a neighborhood gone bad. The yard is without a lawn. Tuffs of grass or a ragweed spruce is all that is growing. Where there once was a chain link fence, only the framing and poles remain. I climb rotting wood steps onto a porch that is just as rotten. I make toward the door. I have a real fear of falling through the slats. They creak with each step.

I ring the doorbell, but hear nothing. With the condition of the place, there is nothing that leads me to think that the doorbell is actually in working order. I resort to knocking on the door in hopes of rousting someone. A short time after, a man comes to the door wearing a T-shirt and a pair of boxer shorts. He's unshaven and holding a can of malt liquor in his hand.

"Yeah," is his greeting.

"I'm looking for the lady of the house, Ms. Jenkins," I reply.

"What, you sellin' somethin'?"

"No. I'm here about what happened to her daughter, Mary."

"You a cop?"

"A private investigator. Is Ms. Jenkins in?"

"Yeah, hold up." The man pushes the door to and leaves me wondering if he's coming back. A few minutes later a short stout woman comes to the door wearing a robe. It's Mary's mother all right. The attractive resemblance is noticeable.

"Yeah, what is it?" She asks crankily.

"Ms. Jenkins, my name is Mick Hart. First, I would like to say I'm sorry for your loss. I'm a private investigator hired by someone to look into the death of your daughter."

"What is it you looking for?"

"Just some background information. Do you have a minute?" Ms. Jenkins answered by opening the door wider allowing me access to come inside.

I might have given a second thought to coming inside if I knew that the condition of the inside of the house was not much better than the outside. A stale stench fills my nostrils. It almost chokes me. The house is cluttered with clothes, newspapers and other odds and ends that didn't seem to belong together. The furniture has rips and torn patches repaired with what appears to be black electrical tape.

An adult roach sees that there is company and heads towards the back of the house. Perhaps he's getting me something to drink. I pretend not to see it, while keeping an eye out for its return. Ms. Jenkins pushes through the cluttered room and makes space for me to sit on the couch. She grabs a blanket and a pillow from the couch and tosses them aside. On the coffee table, there is junk mail ads, coupons for KFC specials, as well as, several open cans of Colt 45 acting as paperweights. In the midst of my surveying, without warning, she lights into me.

"What the fuck do you want! Did that muthafucka from her job send you over here, so he don't have to give me any money?" demands Ms. Jenkins

"Excuse me. I don't know who you're talking about." I defend.

"I told his sorry ass that he owed me some money. Mary was working for his ass and he *shoulda* had some kinda insurance on her."

"Whoa, whoa. Who are you talking about?"

"Jack Daniel, the man she was working for. I told him I needed some money to pay for Mary's funeral. She was working for him, he shoulda had some type of insurance on her."

"Just to set things straight, I don't know any Jack Daniel and I'm not here on his behalf. Is that why no one has claimed the body from the police?"

"Damn right. The undertaker won't go get the body without getting paid up front. Sorry ass."

While Ms. Jenkins continues her lament about how the neighborhood's white mortician owes the black community a free funeral for those who can't afford it, I try to remember what it was that had me take this case. Ah yes, I promised the suspected killer's mother three days of investigation. Three free days of my time to prove that Perry Rogers didn't kill Mary Jane Jenkins, something that even I don't believe. And at this point, I don't care one way or the other. I just want to leave. Before I can do so, the roach is returning along the wall, but it doesn't have my drink.

My attention is brought back to Mrs. Jenkins when she stands from the couch and her robe falls open. Underneath, she is breast naked as a low bosom swings into view. I look. She is slow to cover. Eventually, the robe closes to conceal Ms. Jenkins' nakedness. Our eyes meet and she just stares. I'm trying to recall her last words and nothing comes clear. "Sorry ass" is all I can remember her saying.

"Ms. Jenkins, is there any other family members that could help you with the funeral costs?"

"Hell naw. My family ain't got no money and her sorry ass father left me a long time ago."

"This may sound strange, but what about Perry Rogers' family?"

"Yeah right. You must not know, he's the one the police said killed her."

"Do you think he did it?"

"He could have. He is one of them nerdy types, like he could be one of those psycho serial killers."

"Why do you say that?"

"He works at a bank. He was always nice to me. That's why I'm sayin'. He could have done it if he became jealous and shit. Cause Mary had a lot of men friend. Not too many men can handle a girl like Mary."

"So you believe that Perry Rogers caught Mary with one of these friends and then killed her?"

"I'm sayin' that it coulda happen. What you tryin' to find out?"

"The truth."

I conclude my conversation with Mrs. Jenkins on that note. Standing on the porch, I'm surveying the neighborhood, when the man of the house still in his underwear joins me.

"Man, I think your boy did it." He offers, while scratching his pubic area.

"Really?" I return as an open-ended question.

"Yeah, that Mary was something else. Hell, if she offered me some, I'da took it and gave her whatever she wanted. I could see a niggah killin' somebody over her. And I could see a niggah killin' her if he caught her cheatin'. That girl was something else."

"Do you know any of Mary's friends?"

"Nah. Mary kept her shit tight. Not too many people knew her business. No real girlfriends to speak of. Not until this dude came along who was goin' to marry her, the other niggahs came and went. You know how mutha fuckas are. Hit it and quit it."

"Yeah."

What I took away from my visit with Mrs. Jenkins and her friend is there seemed little to no sorrow felt in Mary's passing. Ms. Jenkins seemed to be angrier at not being able to get some kind of financial compensation than over losing a daughter. If anything at all, Mrs. Jenkins male friend probably views Mary's dying as a missed opportunity.

There has to be someone who is sadden by Mary's death.

~~~~~~~

A short drive across town brings me to the address and home of Teri Jenkins, the older sister of Mary Jane Jenkins. Teri Jenkins now has temporary custody of Sapphire and Gerald, Mary's children. Teri's home and neighborhood is upscale compared to that of her mother's. I am thankful for that, as I watch kids at play in the front of the house. There is a mix of boys and girls making it difficult to pick out Mary's children.

"My name is Mick Hart. I'm an investigator." I introduce myself to the attractive woman who answers the doorbell.

"Shit!" she replies. The woman is Teri Jenkins by the family resemblance. Teri is an older and prettier version of her sister Mary. She's carrying a baby on one hip of her about 5' 3", compact 120 pounds body frame. Following her into the house to the living room, I can see that she is a physically solid specimen of a woman. The stirrup stretch pants are clung tightly to her curvaceous lower body.

"Have a seat Mr. Hart. Are you from Section Eight?"

"No."

"I heard one these bitches around here called the Housing Authority about me having temporary custody of my sister's kids. With my four kids and her two, I'm in violation of my lease. If you not from the Housing Authority, what you investigating me for?"

"Actually, I'm looking into your sister's death."

"I thought the police had Perry for killin' my sister."

"They do. I'm just following up on some other leads." I'm lying; there are no other leads. "Do you think Perry Rogers killed your sister?"

"I guess. I was surprised though. He seemed like he really loved her."

"How much do you know about what the police have on Perry?"

"They have the knife he killed her with."

"Did you know someone else may have been in the house?"

"No."

"Do you know any of your sisters' other male friends?"

"No. We haven't been close."

"But, you have her children."

"That's because my mother didn't want them."

"Has anyone talked to the children about the night their mother died?"

"I was told that I shouldn't bring it up. So I haven't."

"And they haven't volunteered anything. Do they seem bothered by it?"

"Not really. Sapphire is quieter than usual. Gerald never does talk much."

"Do you think they saw anything?"

"I thought they were sleep?"

"Yeah. I'm just following up."

"I doubt they would tell anything anyway. My sister *kicked it* with quite a few guys. For her to keep her game tight, she had to have her kids under control, if you know what I mean. They don't see nothing, they don't hear nothing and they don't say nothing."

"That's a shame."

"Why?"

"Because someone could be getting away with murder."

IV.   Kickin' It with Mary, Again (Perry)

"Insanity is continuing to do the same things and hoping for different results." ~ *Unknown*

It was a mistake for me to make my way back into Mary's arms and bed. Especially after I partially paid for an abortion of the child she was carrying. No, it wasn't mine. That is not to say that I didn't have opportunity for it to be mine. The sex was the part of the relationship that made it hard to let go. By the only other term I can think of, the woman was "sexually uninhibited." I say this, not only because of the different kinds of sex we had, but the talent Mary had.

Mary's body was so soft and supple. She's one hundred and eighty some odd pounds of smooth baby fat. Whether it is baby fat still with her from birth, or gained from the two kids of her own, it doesn't matter. Her thighs remind me of fresh baked Krispy Kreme donuts, soft and warm and my face was ready to be covered with glaze. Yes, the sex hooked me initially, but in the time I had been with Mary, I had grown to genuinely care for her and her two children Sapphire and Gerald.

My caring for Mary was based on the potential I saw in her. The pure sense of affection that she exuded and her intense passion when we embraced told me that she was capable of love. When we talked, she told me of her dreams to have a comfortable, worry free life for her and her kids. She didn't possess dreams of grandeur, just dreams to have a car to get around, a home of her own and money to feed her family. Not once had her dreams involved a man. I didn't take personal exception to that. I did ask myself, then "why am I here." Also, the new found feelings I had for Mary hadn't made it any easier dealing with her thoughtlessness, when it came to her dealings with me.

Let me give some background on me. I am a third line bank manager, who makes decent money. Professional and sophisticated women surround me all day long. Not to toot my own horn, but I have these same women asking me out to lunch on a regular basis. I hadn't gotten into a serious relationship with any of them because of the games most of them play. When they aren't playing games, I find some of these college graduates to be knuckleheads. Most of the time I lose at this dating game or *"kickin' it"* because I play by a different set of rules. Actually, Mary played by a different set of rules too, hers.

I'm from the old school. I treat a woman like a lady, paying for lunches and dinners, buying her flowers and small token gifts. What do I get in return? Dissed. "I can buy my own lunch and dinner." "No one told you to buy me this tennis bracelet, but thank you though." This is what I get for being a nice guy to these so called 'millennium women.' Then these same superficial women will come crying on my shoulders when they have lost a bout of the dating game, after Mr. Wrong has had his turn at play. *Kickin' it* is cool until you are the one kicked. I'm through with it. Well, almost.

We all have baggage that we carry with us from past relationships. You just heard mine. When it came to Mary, I feel that if given the chance to show her sincere love and affection, I could've won her over and made a change in her life. I don't plan to be anymore than myself or do anymore than I would normally do to show someone that I care. As a start, I cut back on the booty calls with Mary and start spending quality time during the daylight hours getting to know her outside the bedroom.

Nights of dancing and eating out was a refreshing change to sitting around Mary's two-bedroom apartment. Both of us were introduced to new experiences and places. I took Mary to some of the upscale restaurants in the city. For the first time, Mary had lobster. "This thing look like it wants to eat me." She loved it. Instead of her regular E&J brandy at the bar, I introduced Mary to Courvossier. "Hell, I can get a whole bottle of E&J for what you're paying for a glass for this stuff," was her impression of the cognac. To enrich Mary culturally, I took her to jazz festivals, art shows and poetry readings. She told me, "you are the whitest, black person I know." I wasn't sure if that was a compliment or not.

As I said, the new experiences came from both sides. Despite my efforts, Mary and her kids still loved their fast food. The kids were well skilled in fast food self-service. Mary would order the kids food and two cups for water. Sapphire and Gerald knew to go to the soda fountain machine and pretend to get water, but instead they would fill their cups with soda. Not just any soda, they knew to select one that was clear to keep up the appearance. You can save a lot of money when you shop at the Save-A-Lot and Family Dollar stores. Mary fed her family on a hundred and fifty dollars worth of groceries to last close to a month. That is what I spend on groceries every two weeks, not counting lunches out. When it came to finding places to party, Mary knew. From smoke filled hole in the wall bars, to off-the-hook all night dance clubs, Mary knew them all and the people there knew Mary.

Outside the Quality nightclub, some guy driving a black Ford Explorer called Mary over to his SUV. She told me she would be right back. Right back was thirty minutes longer than I would have liked. We argued about her show of disrespect to me as her date. All she had to say in her defense was that "I was tripping."

"Listen Mary, you need to make a decision about me and this relationship. Either you are with me or you aren't."

"What are talking about? I am with you. But that don't mean you own me." Mary shot back.

"We're not talking about anyone owning you. It's about showing me respect."

"You just like the rest of them, bein' insecure and shit."

"WHAT THE HELL IS WRONG WITH YOU? HOW ARE YOU GOING TO TRY TO TURN THIS AROUND ON ME? YOU NEED TO START TAKING RESPONSIBILITY FOR YOUR ACTIONS."

"Who do you think you yelling at? You act like we married. We ain't married and you don't have no papers on me, no kids by me, no nothing!"

"YOU! YOU . . . you need to understand that unless you change your behavior, nothing is going to change for you. Have you ever thought that if I'm not the only guy who felt insecure about being with you, then maybe it's you that is causing it?"

"OH, so what you going to do, beat my ass too . . . just because I was talking to some guy?"

"What? Hell naw. I don't believe in hitting women. I'd rather walk away."

That's what I thought to do. Just walk away. As we lay in bed that night, Mary told me of the guy who beat her within an inch of her life because of his insecurity. She was in the hospital for a week. I didn't know what to say. All I could do was hold her tender, supple, full body in my arms. I thought that was the worst that there could be until I noticed a thin line on Mary's neck. In an attempt to change the subject, I asked her did she have her tonsils taken out.

"No." she replied.

"Then what is this mark on your neck?"

"That's from when Sapphire's daddy raped me. That's how I got pregnant with her. He held a knife to my throat."

I didn't want to know, but then again I did. The vision of some man lying atop of Mary with a knife at her throat filled my thoughts. Then my analytical mind offered a diversion. She said Sapphire's daddy raped her. That meant Gerald was by a different man. Do I dare ask? One diversionary question brought me an unsuspected response. Being an analytical man, I had to know.

"Where is Gerald's father?"

"In jail."

Damn! I silently exclaim. "What did he do?"

"He was one of Sapphire's father's boys. He would come around and we would kick it and stuff. Then one night, he decided that he wanted to rape me too. So he did."

I felt sick to my stomach. A lump in my throat grew to a size that almost choked me. My eyes began to water and I didn't know why. The more I got to know Mary as she opened up to me, the more I wish she hadn't. The story of rapes and sexual abuse from her mother's boyfriends carried on through the night. Mary never cried as she relived the painful memories. But I did. I cried because I was angry and I cried for Mary, perhaps she couldn't.

I didn't run away from Mary. That would have been wrong. I remained by her side, whether that meant being a friend, a lover, or whatever she needed. This may sound insane or selfish. But, I thought if I was there to have sex with Mary whenever she wanted it, there would be no opportunity or need for some other man to come into her life to abuse, use or misuse her as others had done in the past.

Gerald and Sapphire began looking forward to my visits. I looked forward to seeing them as well. Sapphire was the first of the two children to accept me. She loudly announced me when I was at the door and greeted me with a hug and a kiss. We played a game that she was my little girlfriend and that her mother was my big girlfriend. Gerald was still a little standoffish. There were a few times when I saw a glint of happiness on his face when I would tell them to get their jackets, "we're going out." I like kids. That included Mary's kids. For the most part they were well mannered.

The idea of a ready-made family was appealing. Sapphire, six and Gerald five had them in the molding years. After three months of being in their lives, they listened to me and obeyed me when I chastised them. We got along great. They began inquiring whether I was going to stay the night or not.

"Not tonight. I'm thinking about going to church in the morning." I told Sapphire.

"I wanna go to church with you." She informed me.

I looked to Mary who said Sapphire could go. Gerald said that he wanted to come along. Mary didn't volunteer to join us. I didn't try to persuade her one way or the other. I knew it was a personal decision that she had to make on her own. Mary's only comment or expressed thought about church was about the fashion show that goes on there. That was an argument that I wasn't going to take on.

On the way to church, the children and I listened to gospel music on the radio. Sapphire sat in the front seat. She enjoyed taking the place of her mother. They loved it when Kirk Franklin and Nu Generation's "Stomp" came on. I turned up the volume and we would yell "STOMP" in unison with the choir. Even Gerald joined in. Children are beautiful gifts to be shared.

Again, the thought of being a part of a family entered my mind. I was a few blocks away from the church. That didn't stop me from getting an early start on a prayer that was on my heart. I asked God for some guidance in this situation and to help *me*. Then a song came on the radio that told me I was praying for the wrong thing, and for the wrong person. Mary and her children didn't need me. The song's chorus, "someone needs you, more than I. So I pray, Lord hear them when they cry." "More Than I", *Luther Barnes & The Red Budd Gospel Choir* the disc jockey announced at the end of the song. It would take more than me to make a difference in Mary's life. But if allowed, I might be able to positively influence the children. I was willing to try.

Later that evening I hugged Gerald and gave him a soft punch in his chest, and then I tucked him in bed. Sapphire waited anxiously for her turn.

"Good night girlfriend," I told the little girl.

"Good night boyfriend," she replies. Then she asks, "Are you going to marry my mommy?"

"Why are you asking me that?"

"Because I want you to be my daddy."

"Well, that depends on what your mommy wants."

"Don't tell her I asked you, okay?"

"Why?"

"Cause she told me to stay out of her business."

"I won't tell her. Good night little girlfriend."

In bed, waiting on Mary to join me, the crossroad of where do we go from here was before me. The kids like me, I like them. I have very little idea what was up with Mary. She took everything I offered. In return, I go to sleep with a smile on my face, a tingling sensation throughout my body and pillow softness lying next to me. Is that all that Mary was to me? That was all she had shown. I felt that, if given the opportunity, I could provide for her and the children all their needs and many of their wants.

I had a business trip out of town for a week. The night before leaving, we made love as if I was going off to war. That's when it happened. It slipped out and I didn't care. There was no reaction from Mary, so did that mean she didn't care either. We didn't break our rhythm and no mention was made of my saying, "I love you."

Something had indeed happened though. While away, when I called Mary, she always seemed preoccupied or she was short on talking. When I would call her late after I got to my hotel room, she didn't answer the phone.

The night I arrived back in Odelot from my trip, I went by Mary's to drop off some items I picked up for the kids. Parked in front of Mary's apartment was a familiar SUV, a black Ford Explorer. Music was coming from inside. I knocked on the door for twenty minutes, no one came to answer. I hung the gifts on the doorknob, turned and walked away . . . never to return again.

V.   Oh Mary Mac (Mick)

As educated and well-read as Perry Rogers appears, when trying to understand women, he is as dumb as men come. All Rogers had to do was pick up a women's magazine every once in and a while and read. I do. Personally, I like smelling the perfume samples. Besides that, the magazines are filled with keen insight into what women want. In Rogers' case, he would have benefited greatly by reading such articles as "Thug Passion: Loving a Roughneck" or "Why Smart Women Love Jerks" and "Some Good Girls Prefer Bad Boys."

At this point, it would be presumptuous of me to call Mary Jane Jenkins a smart woman or a good girl. Yet she seems to have exhibited all the characteristics of the women who fall for the wrong kinds of guys and not appreciate the good guy when he is staring her in the face. Perry Rogers on the other hand, knew exactly what he was dealing with and he made the decision to remain involved.

Perry was for all intents and purposes what women considered a "good guy." He's caring and sensitive, and a provider. Women like Mary eat guys like Perry alive. They would rather be dogged, disciplined and taken advantage of by bad boys. At the same time, women think they can convert these bad boys and make them into someone else. Once you remove the dangerous element, and the rough exterior of these bad boys, what do you have left, someone like Perry Rogers?

The nightclub where Mary encountered the guy in the Ford SUV is called The Quality. There is where I begin looking for someone who may help cast reasonable doubt on Perry Rogers being Mary's killer. The Quality Club is what is considered a hole-in-the wall. Four walls, a bar, a small tiled section considered a dance floor and a few card tables and chairs. It isn't a place where I would think a young woman like Mary would hang out. After seeing the bar filled with older men with younger women on their arms, it's conceivable that Mary came to the club in the company of a Sugar Daddy. More than likely, Mary considered the older male patrons of the bar, easy pickings. Johnny Taylor's "Good Love" is playing on the jukebox.

I take a seat at the small bar and order myself a Rum and Coke. Behind the bar, serving drinks is a middle-aged woman who looks worst for her wears. She has a Tina Turner cut hairstyle that looks uncombed. The T-shirt the woman is wearing is tightly stretched over some oversized busts. She says her name is Betty, flashing a top row of capped teeth. Actually, they could be the uppers of a pair of dentures. Betty keeps smiling, giving me every opportunity to decide between caps or dentures. I smile nicely in return, making small talk, before I try to enlist her help.

"You got a pretty good crowd tonight." I state.

"Yeah. It's Friday and the first of the month. These old fools got their paychecks for those who work and the others have their Social Security money burning a hole in their pockets. Soon enough, they will be pissy drunk and broke. It's the same thing every month. They come in here with some *hoochie* on they arms, spending all they money trying to impress 'em," replies Betty.

"You think they would learn."

"Yeah well, half of 'em can't do nothin' anyway. They ain't thinkin' with the right head if you ask me and that Viagra done gone to that one. Hey, I made a funny."

"Yeah that was cute. And they say money can't buy you love."

"That ain't love they buyin'. It's lust. So what are you lookin' for?"

"I'm looking for which one of these guys might have been buying some love from this woman." I show Betty a photo of Mary.

"Oh, that's Mary Mac. I never knew her full name. That's what I call her, cause she's always dressed in black when she comes in. What are you five-O?"

"No. I'm a private investigator. I'm trying to gather some background information on her."

"What for?"

"She's dead."

"NO!" Outwardly disturbed, Betty drops a bottle of Jim Beam on the bar. I position the bottle upright to stop the spillage. "Poor child. She was such a nice girl. Oh my God. How did it happen?"

"Someone killed her."

"Jesus!"

"Did Mary come here often?"

"Two or three times a month."

"Did she come alone?" Betty's teeth are undetectable.

"Frank wouldn't hurt that girl."

"Frank?"

"I ain't sayin' nothin' else. I think you ought to be goin'."

"Betty, I told you I wasn't the police. I just want to find out what kind a woman Mary Jane Jenkins was."

"She was a good girl. Now, I have customers."

"Betty."

"TONY!" Betty yells across the bar. I look in the direction of where she's looking to see a mountain of a man moving towards us. How could I have missed such an enormous member of the human species in this small bar? I put both hands in the air to signal I surrender before the battle begins. "Tony, he needs to be shown the door."

"Thanks Tony, but I think I can find the door on my own." I pull out a business card and lay it on the bar. Tony grabs it a tosses it in the middle of the crowded room. I make my way to the door chancing a look back at Betty. As I had hoped, she is watching me leave.

Sitting outside the club, I'm watching for every black Ford Explorer that passes and parks, taking down their license plate numbers. There are three. Tomorrow, I will have my assistant Verna to look up the license and get names of the registered owners.

~~~~~~~

None of the SUVs are registered to anyone with the first name of Frank. I decide to follow up with a visit to each owner. The first guy is a security guard who said he didn't know Mary. The second SUV and address was that of Carla Sykes, who works as a school administrator. As it turns out, her husband was stealing the keys and driving the vehicle to the bar. She wasn't aware, but boy did she let him have it when I inquired. Lastly, there is Anthony James.

After a half day stake out of the address Verna gave me, Anthony or the black SUV is a no show. The address is that of his mother's house. Mrs. James an elderly woman who says she hasn't seen her only son in a week. Anthony James has a street name of Smoke. He's a hustler. That's what I gathered from asking around. Anthony is what I call a welfare pimp. He makes his rounds every first and fifteenth of the month, laying up with women on welfare and receiving Social Security checks. These women will take food out of their children's mouths and clothes off their backs to feed and buy for these welfare pimps. It makes me sick to my stomach.

I drive through the city's projects and low income area looking for a late model black Ford Explorer with matching license plate numbers to those of one Anthony James, a.k.a. Smoke. Nothing. I might as well follow-up on another name on my checklist, Jack Daniel.

I pull into the dirt and gravel paved parking lot of JD's Marketing Group. On the lot is a double wide trailer serving as the office building. JD's Marketing Group is owned and operated by Jack Daniel. Jack was Mary's boss. I called Jack letting him know I want to talk with him. JD as he calls himself said he would be late, but he would be glad to meet with me.

According to Perry, Jack Daniel used money in incremental raises as payment for sexual favors from his employees, well at least, from Mary. Outside, the tool-shed buildings are several people gathered, smoking cigarettes. I figure I'll start on the outside and work my way in.

"Hey, is the boss in?" I throw out to the group of smokers.

"Why don't you go inside and ask?" throws back an oversized black woman in an undersized clothing outfit. The others turn waiting for my return.

"I thought I might save myself a trip."

"Well *naw*, he ain't here. He ain't hardly ever here."

"I see. Did any of you know Mary Jane Jenkins?"

"Why?" The woman spits at me.

"I'm doing some background research on her. I understand she worked here."

"Yeah, she worked here alright. Like Monica Lewinsky worked at the White House." The other smokers break into a robust laugh in response to the woman's endorsement.

"Cute. So she got along well with Mr. Daniel is what you're telling me?"

"I ain't sayin' nothin. You ain't heard shit from me. Hell, get my ass fired over some he say she say shit. I'm sorry she dead and all, but God don't like ugly and you reap what you sow." The others nod their amen. All put out their smokes and head in the building. I detain Miss Clothes Too Tight.

"Look, I'm just trying to find out what I can about Mary Jane Jenkins and anyone who might have wanted to see her dead. Did she get along with her co-workers?"

"What you tryin' to say?"

"I just want to know if there was anyone in particular that Mary Jane Jenkins might have had trouble with or might have been jealous of the special relationship she had with Mr. Daniel."

"HELL NAW! Don't nobody want that crooked dick man."

"And how would you know he has a crooked dick?"

"Anyway, if you lookin' for somebody to get in trouble, you need to get his ass. I ain't goin' to lie about it. I fucked him a couple of times. Once for a Christmas bonus and again, so I could get my kids school supplies. I got three of 'em at home. I ain't shamed."

"I see. So what can you tell me about Jack and Mary?"

"Like I said, I can't be getting caught up in no bullshit and lose my job."

"This will be between you and me."

"Yeah, I done heard that before too."

"I know you don't know me, but I give you my word."

"Fuck your word. How about some green?" I pull out a couple of twenties and hand them to her. "Hmmmph. Anyway, I hear he got her pregnant. That's why I stop fuckin' him, because he wanted to do it bareback. I'm like hell naw. I can't be havin' no more kids, *specially* by no married man. That's probably why Mary was goin' off on him one day in his office. Right after then she quit."

"Do you think she threatened to tell his wife?"
"I don't even know. Ah SHIT!"

A large late model Oldsmobile pulls into the parking lot. It's too late for the big woman to quickly scamper away. She stays put and we wait for the big man to depart from his car. JD is a big man, as in girth. Once exited his car, it takes him five minutes to pull around his waist, to hoist his pants up. My informant friend jovially greets him.

"HEY JD! How you doin'?"
"Nina, you out here killin' yourself with them cancer sticks?"
"JD, you know I cain't help it."
"You best find a way. Yo' habit is killin' you and my pockets. You suppose to be on that phone makin' me some money."
"Yeah, that's all you really care about; your business and your money."
"Now baby you know that ain't true. I care about you too, cause you are my business."
"Umm, hmmm." All while Nina was talking, she strutted so that whatever part of her she had to poke out from her body, she made sure it did. I quickly gathered that Nina wasn't too sad in seeing Mary either quit her job or quit breathing. After all, school would be starting soon.

"Mr. Daniel, my name is Mick Hart. We spoke on the phone." I extend my hand to the big man.
"Oh yeah. Let's go in to my office." He shakes my hand with a strong grip. We enter Daniel's trailer building. JD's Marketing Group is a tele-marketer selling long distance phone service. On one side of the building is a large room of small cubicles set up to be a call center. Each cubicle is equipped with a phone and computer. On the other half of the trailer, a young, pretty girl sits at a small desk right outside Daniel's office.
"Morning Mr. JD," the young woman greets him.
"Morning Rachel. Any messages?"
"No sir. It's been quiet."
"Good. Bring me coffee, would you honey. How about you Mr. Hart?"
"No thank you."

"Make mine black Rachel."
"Sure JD."

Inside the large office, we each take our seats on our respective sides of a big and paper-cluttered desk. On the walls are outdated certificates and plaques of quality service and performance. The piece of furniture that is out of place is a full sized couch against a wall. I dare guess why it is a part of the decor.

"So what can I do for you Mr. Hart. You said something about a background check on one of my employees," asks Daniel.
"Yes. What can you tell me about Mary Jane Jenkins?"
"IF YOU ARE HERE ON ACCOUNT OF THAT FOUL MOUTH MOTHER OF HER'S, YOU CAN JUST GET OUT! I told that woman she can't sue me because of an accident."
"What accident?" I asked.
"You know damn well what I'm talkin' about. What, you tryin' to get me to say it on tape or somethin'?"
"No, Mr. Daniel. I assure you I'm not taping you. What accident are you referring to?"
"I'm talkin' about Mary gettin' knocked up."
"You got Mary pregnant?"
"That's what she claimed. I tells her it ain't mine and I wasn't payin' the bill for no abortion either."
"So you admit to having sexual relations with one of your employees?" A pause came just as the receptionist Rachel comes in the office with Daniel's cup of coffee. He and I sit quietly staring across the desk at one another. Neither of us pays any attention to the receptionist's presence until she was apparently gone by the sound of the door closing behind her.
"What do you mean employees? Who you been talkin' to?"
"Well, it's obvious that you and Mary were sexually involved. Otherwise, she couldn't make the claim. The question is, was the sex consensual or under duress?"
"What do you mean duress?"
"Did Mary have sex with you under force, pressure, or threat?"
"Ain't nobody threaten that girl. She wanted it."

"Sure she did, but for what in return. Sex for pay is considered a crime."

"Who says I paid her for sex?"

"No one. How often are your employees entitled to a raise?"

"Every six months. Why?"

"It would be interesting to see how frequently Mary received a raise in her wages."

"I don't know what you're talking about."

"Don't play me for stupid Daniel. Clinton didn't get away with it and you won't either. All I need to do is place a few phone calls to the right people and your business will be investigated by everyone from the EEOC to the IRS."

"Okay! Okay! What is it you're after Hart?"

"I'm sure your wife doesn't know you're having sex with your female workers over on that couch." It only takes a little bit of a hunch that will make a person believe you know a lot more than you do. Daniel's eyes dart to the couch. "And the Department of Labor would be very interested in looking at your books and pay raise and bonus practices. I wonder how many other women would be willing to testify to the goings on around here?"

"What do you want?"

"I want you to help with Mary's burial."

"What?"

"You heard me. Nothing fancy, but I want you to call her mother with an offer."

Daniel sits quietly, not moving a muscle. If he calls my bluff, I may have to throw in my hand. All I have is the threat. Nina would be doubtful to testify against her 'bread and butter.' If she were the only other one that old Jack was sticking it to, then that would be my only trump card. After a good five minutes, Jack speaks.

"She was beautiful."

"Excuse me?"

"Mary, she was a beautiful girl . . . inside and out. She gave me experiences I never had with any other woman. I've had my share of women, some professionals if you know what I mean. None of them could hold a candle to Mary. And Mary, she had a voice like an angel."

Jack reaches to the corner of his desk, pressing a button on his phone. A recording begins playing. The voice is light and sweet. "You have reached the office of JD's Marketing Group. Our office hours are from nine to five, Monday through Friday and nine to one on Saturday.

If you would like to leave a message, please wait until the tone. Thank you and have a good day."

Leaving Jack sitting in his office sobbing, he agreed to help with Mary's funeral costs. He confessed to genuinely loving Mary. It wasn't just the sex. Jack said Mary made him feel every bit of a man that he wished he was. "No other woman did that for me," he concluded.

VI. Kickin' It and Screamin' With Mary (Perry)

"God knows how much you can bear, . . . so bend, don't break."

It was after 1:00 a.m. when the doorbell chimed. I wasn't expecting any company, other than Vanessa. I was holding her in my arms at the time. We had just returned from a romantic Friday night out. We attended the *Rhythm of Love* concert tour, featuring Will Downing, Chante' Moore, Gerald Allbright and Phil Perry. I paid $45 a ticket to get a table in the orchestra pit of the amphitheater. Because the event was being held outside at a park, we were allowed to pack a picnic basket. I bought a bottle of Merlot. We packed smoked salmon and crackers with capers and cream cheese spread. The weather matched the hot and steamy performance on the stage. I took some ice from the cooler and placed it on Vanessa's neck, which brought a look of "oh yeah, you know what to do for me" from her. In my home, I confirmed that look by showing Vanessa I did indeed know what to do for her.

Yet, the sounding chimes weren't to be denied. Someone was ringing my doorbell. The light on the front porch cast a shadow on three figures, one adult size and two smaller persons. Opening the door, I discovered Mary, my former lover, Sapphire, my little girlfriend and her brother Gerald, my challenger. Mary's face was battered and bruised. My little girlfriend Sapphire had sleepy eyes. Gerald was dead eyed with an emotionless expression.

How ironic that I was beckoned from my couch and the comfort of the arms of a woman, when the last time I stood at Mary's door, she didn't bother to answer when I pounded. Parked outside of her apartment, was a black SUV belonging to a booty caller. *Kickin' it* music came from inside the apartment. That was the last time I darkened her doorway. I swore that I would never go back.

I had said that I would never go back once before, right after I gave Mary money to help pay for an abortion. The baby wasn't mine and neither was Mary. So, why did I do it? It's complicated. In short, I thought it was best for the unborn baby. Well, I guess I stayed true to my word. I didn't go back, Mary had come to me.

"Do you have any money?" Mary asked

"What do you mean coming by here at this time of morning, bringing these kids with you to ask me for money?" I answered.

"It's not for me, it's to pay for the cab. I need someplace to stay."

"Don't you have a mother?"

"She wouldn't answer the door. Her boyfriend is over," answered Sapphire. Her mother smacked her in the mouth. Sapphire's eyes quickly welled, but she did not allow a tear to spill. She was a strong little girl. I thought that Mary would be the last to be smacking someone in the face given her present condition.

"You talk too much little girl," Mary said to the teary eyed child. Then she turned to me and asked, "Do we have to talk about this right here?"

I looked at the tired eyes of the children, that's what drove my hands into my pocket to retrieve a twenty-dollar bill to hand to Mary. I ushered the kids in, showing them to my den. Vanessa met me in the hall. The look on her face was beyond bewildered. With her mouth agape and hands on her hips, I knew I had some explaining to do.

"It's not what you think. These kids belong to a friend, a woman I know." I explained.

"And what, she dropped them off for you to baby-sit?" Vanessa wanted to know.

"No, she's coming right back."

"Oh really."

"I think they had a family emergency and need my help."

"Oh, I see."

Mary walked in. "Where are the kids?"

"In the den." I replied, which sent Mary on her way to join them.

"What she can't speak?" asked Vanessa.

"I suppose she has other things on her mind."

"That's no excuse to be rude. So just what kind of friend is she, are you two sleeping together?" The question caught me off guard. I didn't want to lie, but I took offense to the question.

"No." We had, and it was fantastic, but Vanessa didn't need to know that. Beside, my sleeping with Mary was in the past and irrelevant to my showing good will to her and the children.

"Yeah, I bet. I knew there was something about you that wasn't right. We've been working together for months and you never looked at me twice until now. That's because you're rebounding from being with Miss Attitude in there. Those kids are probably yours. And just think, I was going to give you *some* tonight." Vanessa walked away, gathered her belongings and left.

I turned off the porch light when Vanessa reached her car. Joining my guess in the den, I found the kids falling asleep on my couch, while Mary watched music videos. She didn't bother looking at me. I decide to hold back on the barrage of questions that I had for her until after I put to kids to bed.

"I suppose we ought to get them into bed." I stated.

Mary yells at them to get up. The children jump to. I ask them to follow me; Mary doesn't bother to help. After seeing to it that they used the bathroom, I tucked them into the same bed in my guestroom. I gave them each a T-shirt to sleep in. Gerald is fast asleep once his little head hits the pillow. As I tuck Sapphire in, she reaches up, squeezes me about the neck, and tells me she loves me. We kiss on the lips and I say goodnight to her. It was close to three in the morning. I was tired and now frustrated that my night had been interrupted.

"You can sleep in my bed." I informed Mary.

"Where are you going to sleep?"

"On the couch."

"Why?"

"Because I want to."

Yes, I am a man, but even I knew that sleeping with Mary that night would only complicate matters. If sex between us would occur, it would be for me to relieve the frustration of missing out on the opportunity to sleep with Vanessa. As for Mary, she probably thought she owed it to me for allowing her to spend the night. She didn't owe me and didn't have to pay me with her body.

Saturday morning, my eyes opened to Gerald standing over me.

"What'sup little man?"
"I want to watch cartoons."
"Sure."

I escorted him to the den, turned on the television and handed Gerald the remote. He selected the channel of his choice and became content. I offered breakfast but he declined. I remembered later that it was Sapphire who ate breakfast and not Gerald. So I went in the kitchen and began cooking some bacon and an omelet. It was soon after that Sapphire walked in the kitchen rubbing her eyes.

Sapphire is a mini version of her mother, with her almond shaped eyes and full pouting lips. What is now a beautiful and innocent smile, may one day be beguiling and entrancing, just like that of her mother's. I prepared Sapphire's plate, kissed her on the forehead and left to take her mother breakfast in bed.

Mary slept in her bra and panties. The sight of her partially covered, full-figured body sprawled across my bed excited my libido. I stood for a minute remembering the pleasures that body brought me. Earlier that morning, I was strong enough to resist the temptation. The sight of those big, soft, luscious thighs and 38 double D breast, barely being contained momentarily weakened me.

I placed the plate on the nightstand and sat on the bed. Mary's back was to me. Placing my hand on the all too familiar fleshy hip of hers, instead of shaking her awake, I squeezed and kneaded the softness. From her hip I massaged to her thigh, then back to her plentiful behind. The skin was butter smooth and cotton candy soft. I felt myself becoming aroused. My mind was shut down and my body was on autopilot. Mary began responding to my actions with low moans and slight motions of her body. We began a rhythm to a dance we've both performed before. All was going well until Mary turned to look at me with soft, sultry eyes. Those same eyes were bruised and slightly swollen.

Seeing that reminded me why she was there in my bed in the first place. My genital auto pilot was shut down and a manual override turned on. My hand immediately stopped its progression.

"Hey, I brought you breakfast. Eggs and bacon."

"Is that all." Mary was looking at the prominent sausage in my pants.

"Yeah, I'm afraid so." I lied.

"If you say so." She knew that I did.

"Do you want to tell me how that happened?" Mary sat up and began working on the plate of food.

"I didn't want to do something, so the guy decided to hit me."

"What is it with you and guys beating on you? I mean if they aren't raping you, they're hitting you. I don't mean to sound like I'm defending them or nothing like that, but could you be doing something to bring this upon yourself?"

"LIKE WHAT?" she snapped at me. "JUST BECAUSE I DON'T WANT TO SUCK HIS THANG, I DESERVE TO GET HIT? I don't know what you think of me, but I don't just suck on every guy who wants it. I'm not no hoe."

"I'm not saying you are a hoe. It's just that you must do something to get yourself in the situation where these guys are expecting something."

"I can't help what they expect. It don't mean I have to give it to them."

"I'm just saying that you need to stop messing with guys who are only interested in you for your . . . body." I sounded every bit the hypocrite with that statement, though I enjoyed the sex, I had become interested in Mary for more than the sex. I knew this, which is why I continued. "They need to get to know you and your kids before they get to know you in bed."

"Oh, like you?"

"Yeah, like me. I have accepted you and your children. True, we started out *kickin' it*, but I stuck around afterwards and tried to be there for you and your kids. If you recall, it was you who wasn't satisfied."

I felt the return of the anger I had the night Mary wouldn't answer the door and I recognized the black SUV of a guy who Mary had a prior relationship. This was after she and I began what I considered a relationship. Mary considered it *kickin' it*, which is non-committal and non-monogamous. I began feeling contemptuous toward Mary, thinking she brought the wrath on herself from whoever the guy was. Immediately following the formation of the thought, I felt ashamed. There was no excuse for a man to hit a woman.

Mary asked to borrow my car to retrieve some clothes for her and the kids. The guy in the SUV took Mary's keys to let himself in her apartment whenever he liked. She was going to have the locks changed by the landlord. In the meantime, they would let her in the apartment to get some clothes. Mary also got another twenty dollars out of me, so she could get a touch up on her fake nails. I didn't mind giving her the money so she could have a little time to herself for some pampering. Some special attention could be the best thing for her.

While Mary was gone, the kids and I became reacquainted. There was little effort needed to make Sapphire become comfortable around me again. Gerald on the other hand was a different story. As I mentioned, he was my challenger, along with every other male vying for his mother's attention. After a few piggyback rides and a round of hide-and-go-seek with Sapphire, Gerald decided he wanted to join in. It wasn't long before we were all wrestling on the floor laughing. Kids just want to be kids. They have a lot of energy at the ages of six and seven. Everything with them is "do me" or "do me again." Playing with them allowed the time to slip by unnoticeably. It was mid afternoon by the time I got them to a point of taking a second breath.

Gerald returned to his favorite pass time, watching television. Sapphire was a little more difficult to shake. I was tired from the short night's sleep and early morning rise. I got Sapphire to allow me to shower and take a short nap, while she watched television with her brother. It wasn't long after my head laid on the pillow that I found the comfort of a restful sleep.

Just before falling asleep, I allowed my thoughts to drift to the possibility of my weekends being fulfilled with a family atmosphere. It would be just like when I was growing up. A Family, with mom and dad and the kids. I would show Mary's kids the magic that my father showed me, by making his thumb disappear. The kid's scrapes and bruises would be such, that they could be kissed away by Mary or I and made all better. No shopping trip would be complete, unless a new toy was brought home. For Sapphire and Gerald, I would want their childhood to be filled with spinning around and falling down as their cause for giggles.

For me, I would like for Mary to be a stay-at-home mom to raise the children like my mother. She was at home for me. When the school nurse wanted to reach someone, my mom didn't have to be paged, or she didn't have to beg her boss for some personal time to come see about me.

As my mate, I wanted Mary to be able to talk sports and know what's going on in world news. Not just what's happening on Jerry Springer and Jenny Jones. I want to be able to come home from a hard day's work to a clean house with a hot dinner on the table. When dinner is eaten, I wanted her to be able to serve up dessert in the bedroom. Yes, dessert in the bedroom. Mary's Krispy Kreme donut thighs, soft and warm, melting at the touch. Her thighs, which are delicately, sweetly glazed, butter soft, and mouth watering. If that's too much to ask, then call me greedy. If there was one thing I was sure of about Mary, it was she could satisfy me in the bedroom.

At that moment of my dream state, it was like we were actually engaged in the beginning of intimate relations. My carnal slumber caused a stir in my groin. The vividness of my thoughts was so intense that I could sense the gentle softness and warm sensation of Mary's small hands stimulating my member. The erotic thoughts moved me to such an arousal that I forced my eyes open from my sleep to make sure that it was just a fantasy.

Once awake, to my surprise the gentle kneading and sensation continued. Slowly I opened my eyes, to capture a glimpse of my on-again-off-again girlfriend Mary busy at work or rather at play. Surprise transformed to shock when I saw not Mary giving me the sensual pleasure but Sapphire instead. I sprang to an upright position in the bed, while pushing Sapphire away from between my legs. The momentum pushed her off the bed onto the floor. I wasn't concerned if she were hurt or not. At the top of my lungs I shouted.

"WHAT IN THE HELL DO YOU THINK YOU'RE DOING?" My voice boomed. Sapphire's eyes were wide and brimming with tears. Fear reflected over her entire face.

"I was just *(sniff)* being nice to you like *(sniff)* my mama, becuz I'm your *(sniff)* girlfriend like her." She said through her crying.

"You can't do everything your mother does and you are not my girlfriend. That was just for play. Good girls don't go around doing that."

"But you let my mama do it."

"WHEN DID YOU SEE YOUR MOTHER . . . NEVER MIND. YOU DON'T DO IT. DO YOU HEAR ME?" There were times when Mary and I may have been careless and began *kickin' it* in the living room while we thought the children were asleep.

(Sniffffff) "Yeesss."

"GO TO YOUR ROOM and don't come out except to use the bathroom."

The little girl who was still wearing my T-shirt got off the floor and ran out of the bedroom. I sat on the bed for what seemed to be an eternity. Actually, it was for an hour or so. Guilt paralyzed me. I didn't know what to do or who to turn to for help. I couldn't go to my boys for advice. I couldn't call my mom and tell her. My shame prevented me from even turning to God in prayer for console. Instead, I remained mentally and physically numb, while my mind imprisoned me with my conscious. *"You called her your little girlfriend."* My accusing conscious reminded me. *You tucked her in bed and kissed her on the lips at night."* My mind was relentless.

What had I done? Was it my fault? Was I the cause of what Sapphire was becoming or had become or was it more the case of "like mother, like daughter?" That thought turned my attention to Mary. Where was she? It was now late in the afternoon. She should have been back from the nail salon and her apartment. Should I tell her what had happened? Could I tell her? Would she believe me or suspect me of sexually abusing her child like she had been? What had I done?

Later on that warm Saturday afternoon, the children were in the backyard playing. Sapphire had bounced back from our earlier encounter. She was once again, a child. When Mary finally returned at about five o'clock it was apparent that she was *high* or had been drinking. Her demeanor was jovial and sexy. Just the way I didn't want her to be. So now it was her turn.

"WHERE IN THE HELL HAVE YOU BEEN?" I screamed.

"What's yo' problem? Where did I tell you I was going?" She did have bags of clothes but her nails weren't done.

"You left early this morning and your nails look the same."

"The shop was too crowded and I ran into a friend of mine."

"Male or female?"

"Why?"

"Because I asked, that's why."

"I don't think it's none of yo' business. Like you somebody daddy *up in hearah.*"

"You know, no I'm not your daddy or your man. But you are not going to come in my house, leaving your kids and go out acting like some tramp. You have two kids to be thinking about."

"They was here with you weren't they?" The question brought up a half dozen more with it.

"That is not the point. I am not their father. But you are their mother and you need to be more responsible."

"You men always tryin' to own somebody and control them."

"I'm not trying to control you. I'm trying to tell you what is right."

"I don't appreciate you jumpin' in my face like you goin' to kick my ass or somethin'."

"What are you talking about? I'm not thinking about kicking your ass, though you've given me plenty reasons why I should."

"Yeah right."

"Mary, you are headed down a destructive path. If you don't change your life for you, do it for your kids."

"Why you keep bringin' up my kids? Like you *said*, you ain't their father."

"That's right, I'm not. How do you think it looks to them, with you having a different man going in and out of your bedroom every other week or night?"

"I'm getting' tired of you tryin' to call me a hoe. *You* didn't have a problem comin' and goin' in my bedroom did you?"

"No I didn't and that is not the point. You are now in my house and sleeping in my bedroom. And I'm trying to tell you that there is a better life for you and the kids, in my house. But you need to respect me. Before you respect me, you need to find some respect for yourself."

"I do respect myself. I am a single mother struggling. I do what I *have* to do for me and my kids."

"No Mary, you do what you *want* to do for you."

"How are you goin' to tell me what I'm doin'? You livin' phat and shit in your big house and nice job, while I'm tryin' to work and raise two kids, alone."

"And that's precisely what I'm trying to tell you, you don't have to be alone. You are alone because you choose to mess around with men who may not be there when you wake up the morning. You are alone because your men only come and go in the wee hours of the night or morning. You are alone because you allow these men to do as they please, when they please, and what do you get in return?"

I let the question hang in the air until I saw that its sting caused tears to form in Mary's eyes. Every word I meant so I didn't bother to apologize. Mary pushed passed me and went upstairs. I expected her to gather her kids and things and walk out the door. She didn't. Instead, she stayed in my room the rest of the night.

I fed the kids pizza and had Sapphire take a plate up to her mother. The kids and I watched scary movie videos. When it came to bedtime, I sent them both off. I peeked in on Mary who was watching some movie on cable. I sat on the bed to announce my presence. Mary didn't acknowledge. I didn't feel the need to accentuate my earlier rant by alienating her. I showered and returned to bed as usual; still no acknowledgement.

It wasn't until early morning that I felt Mary cuddle next to me. She pulled my arm around her and placed my hand on a mound of naked flesh. It was pleasing to touch, but that was as much enjoyment I allowed myself. It was difficult fighting the urge to do what would come natural when holding a soft tender voluptuous breast. But I did. Then Mary asked; "what do you want me to do?" Before answering, I laid there for a while caressing and kneading.

"I don't want you to do anything." We lay quietly and spooned together. Mary pushed back into me, nuzzling her ample behind in my crouch. The flesh is weak where the mind is strong. "I've changed my mind, I do want you to do something. Let's just talk, Mary."

"What about?"

"You."

"What about me?"

"Whatever you want to share."

For the next two hours Mary revealed more of her life story. She explained that at an early age (like that of her daughter Sapphire), all men and boys wanted from her was her body. Short of calling herself a hoe, Mary admitted to giving men what they wanted in order to get what she wanted. This included Mary's boss, who gave her a twenty-five cent pay raise for each time he could go to bed with her. The more Mary shared of her life adversities and challenges, the tighter I held her close to me. The things she revealed caused me pain and shame of being a man. The pain eased and the shame subsided with the self-disclosure that I wasn't the kind of man that Mary was used to dealing with. I was not above making mistakes and being a sinner, but I was/am above causing deliberate pain and hurt to someone else for my own selfish needs. My parents and their spiritual guidance taught me to be a decent man. Realizing that, I knew what I had to do.

Sunday morning light came shortly after Mary and I closed our eyes for a few hours sleep. My morning routine was to go out early, buy a Sunday newspaper, stop, and get a cup of coffee at McDonalds. That morning, I bought breakfast for my houseguests and me. I wanted to give them an energetic start to a brand new day. The children were up and eating in the kitchen, including Gerald. I bought him pancakes. When I brought breakfast in bed to Mary, I asked her to eat quickly because I wanted her and the children to go somewhere with me. I wouldn't answer her numerous questions as to where. I ironed all their clothes, while Mary showered the kids and herself.

It was when we became close to our destination did Sapphire announce, "I know where we going. We been here before." Yes, she and Gerald had attended church with me one Sunday before. Mary made objections to going. As it so happened, it was fifth Sunday, which was "come as you are and bring a friend" service. When Mary saw the casual dress of the others, she felt more at eased.

The service order was a call to worship, devotion, invocation, and musical interlude. The more than one hundred member strong choir raised their voices in songs of praise. The first song being, "*God Knows How Much You Can Bear.*" We had the spiritual reading, church announcements, then came the recognition of visitors. Mary looked upon me with a deathly fear, as if Peter himself was calling her to stand before him at the gates of heaven. With the large number of visitors attending church that day, Mary was lost among the hoard of others on this special Sunday. She smiled with a sigh of relief when she sat back down. Offering was taken, while the choir sung "*Bend, Don't Break.*"

The Reverend Isaac M. Lowdown took his place in the pulpit. The church applauded his presence, as he began to offer the word.

"Good morning church." He greeted. Before he actually began the sermon he asked of the congregation: "hug a hundred of your neighbors." The congregation chuckled at the jest, but proceeded to hug as many as they could. I turned to Mary and said, "one."

"We have to hug one hundred people?" She asked sincerely.

"No, just fifty." I answered with a smirk. Gerald and Sapphire were well on achieving their goal of hugs. Mary didn't stray far from our pew, but the open arms of our church members came to her. That is when Mother Johnnie Mae came to us. The church members say that Mother Johnnie Mae is gifted with the sight of prophecy.

Mother Johnnie Mae came to me first with an embrace. She began jerking and shaking while she held me. When she stepped back, she looked me straight away, saying; "It's a beautiful thing you are doing. God is blessing you as you are blessing others." I smiled and thanked her, not fully grasping her words. The Mother looked passed me to Mary. She took hold of Mary and squeezed her in a bear hug. The jerking and shaking commenced, then Mother began speaking in tongue. Looks of fear once again shown on Mary's face.

Mother stopped speaking and began crying and rocking Mary as if she were her child. Her crying was heavy, but she held on to Mary and Mary, too, did not let go. I didn't know what to do. Sapphire and Gerald put their arms around their mother as best as they could. That is when Mary broke down to tears and a lump formed in my throat. Ushers came to attend to Mother, helping her to her seat. She never looked upon Mary's face as she walked away yelling over and over "HALLELUJAH." Sitting next to Mary, I offered her my handkerchief, which she gladly accepted.

"Are you okay?" I asked.

"I guess. What did she do to me?"

"What do you mean?"

"All of the sudden I started feeling warm inside and I just started crying."

"I don't know."

"She didn't put no spell on me did she?"

I laughed. "You are funny."

"Why? I've heard about people in them cults and stuff."

"This is not a cult. This is a church."

"Mmmhmmm."

Reverend I. M. Lowdown returned to the pulpit with an "amen." The congregation responded, "Amen."

"Today's sermon is about *making it through the storm. Can I get an amen*?

"When the Doppler radar tells the weatherman that a storm is coming, he interrupts your regularly scheduled program to tell you the news so you can seek shelter. Instead of taking heed of the warning, many of you become upset at the interruption, depending on the program you are watching. That is how many churchgoers feel about hearing the word of God. You don't want to hear God warning you about the storm that is coming in your life.

"God is the ultimate forecaster, weatherman, and meteorologist. He doesn't need a radar screen. He doesn't lick his finger and stick it in the air to find out which way the storm is coming. God can see the storm past the horizon, past the Doppler radar. When God told Noah to build the ark, there wasn't a cloud in the sky, but God KNEW, a storm was coming. God knows the storms in your lives," spoke the reverend.

"Some of you are in the midst of a storm right now. Some of you are doing fine, but a storm may be forming on the horizon for you. You need to know how to *make it through the storm*. Turn to your neighbor and say, 'making it through the storm.' God sometimes brings a storm into your life. Oh, you done got quiet on me. I said, God sometimes brings a storm into your life.

"We've been having a little bit of stormy weather here in our city, amen. The other day I was sitting in my office when I heard the weatherman say that a storm was headed our way. I didn't pay him no mind, because the weatherman can be wrong, amen. When they say a storm is coming and then it blows over top of us, they want to laugh about it the next day. I paid the weatherman no mind. I looked out my office window at a large tree out back, for God's signs that a storm was coming.

"God uses the same signs when He's telling you that a storm is about to come in your life. Suddenly, a strong breeze came and began rustling the leaves on the tree. That's God sign to the tree that a storm is coming. To you, a strong breeze can be a friend, a loved one, or your pastor. *Hello, is anybody listening?*

"When a young girl's mother tells her to leave that boy alone, because he ain't no good, that's God blowing a strong breeze before a storm hits. When parents tell kids 'don't mess with drugs and alcohol,' that's God blowing a strong breeze before a storm hits. When a friend tells you that you don't have to give yourself to that man in order to receive love in return, that's God blowing a strong breeze before a storm hits. God loves you unconditionally. Man loves you for what you can do for him, but not God. *Am I right about it*?

"When a married man comes home after running around with other women and has a burning and a tingling in his pants, that's . . . *Hello*!

"Sometimes God has to rustle of few leaves on your tree to get you to listen. *It's a shame that that I don't have no saints in here.*

"Like we don't heed the weatherman's warning, we don't listen to God's either. Then it's too late and the storm is upon us. As I watched that tree outside my window, and the storm came through, I saw the leaves break off and dead, weak limbs break loose. That was the power of God getting rid of the dead from the tree. It was His breath that pruned the dead limbs.

"There are people and things in your lives that need to be pruned, broken off, and cast aside. Bad habits, bad relationships, a grudge against someone in your life, these are things that as children of God you need to prune. Break off. By not doing so, you find yourselves in the midst of a storm. God will allow you to weather the storm to rid you of these dead-weighted limbs that keep you from growing closer to him. A dead limb can't grow. Turn to your neighbor and say, 'dead limbs can't grow.' *Can I get an amen?*

"That old tree outside my window weathered the storm. The winds blew it from side to side, backwards and forward. At one point it seemed to bend to the ground, but it CAME BACK STRAIGHT. It didn't fall over. It had strong roots. God's children, brought up in the church also have strong roots in God's word and His love. If you rely on God's love through the storm, you too will bend but you will not break.

"Like the choir sung in their selection this morning, 'no matter what it takes, bend, don't break.' You may be in the midst of a storm but don't worry . . . bend, don't break. With God's love you can weather the storm. Turn to today's scripture Matthew, six and twenty-seven. When you find it say amen. Let us read, *'Which of you by taking thought can add one cubit unto his stature.'* In other words, *'who of you by worrying can add a single hour to his life?*

"While in the midst of the storm, you often let yourselves get preoccupied with worrisome things. What does this get you? Nothing. It hastens your dying.

"Minister of Music, could you have the choir sing more of the song?"

The man sitting at the keyboard raised his hand and the choir stood in response. The musicians began to play while the mass group started to sway in unison and on cue began singing the songs' chorus.

"Lead vocalist: "No Matter"
Choir: "No matter what it takes,"
"No matter what it takes . . . bend, don't break"
"Bend, don't break."
"You can make it, . . . through grace and faith"
"You can make it through grace and faith"
"So hold on, trust and wait"
"Trust and wait"
"Jesus is coming"
"Jesus is coming . . ."
"And he won't be late, can I get a witness"
" . . . And he won't be late"
"Why don't you turn around and tell somebody, bend, don't break?"

"Bend, . . . don't, . . . bend, don't break."

"Let us pray. Father, we thank you. We thank you for making the earth hold its orbit and our hearts to keep its beat. Oh Lord, we thank you for giving us the root of your love and grace to weather the storms in our lives. Forgive us when we don't heed your warnings, Oh Lord. Forgive us when we don't count these blessings in our lives. Thank you Dear Heavenly Father for giving us the will to bend and the strength of your grace and faith not to break. In Jesus name we pray. Amen." The reverend concluded.

On the way home from church that day, Mary was full of questions about the pastor's sermon. She was like a brand new person, a child reborn. She wanted to know what I thought the message meant. I knew exactly what it meant to me. I needed to let loose some dead limbs that weren't allowing me to grow. I looked at Mary, then to Sapphire and Gerald in the backseat. I took a deep sigh.

Like the reverend said, we don't take heed to God's warnings. By the time night fell that fateful Sunday, Mary and I were in bed, in one another's arms. We talked. We laughed. We loved. We kicked it for another month or so after that day, before I proposed marriage to Mary and she accepted. I'm glad we were able to make it through the storm.

VI.   Mary Go Round (Mick)

My investigation brought me back to the curbside a block away from the Quality nightclub. It is a busy night for the club's business. The area filled rather quickly with cars parked everywhere. Fortunately, I have a prime spot to see the club's patrons come and go, so I thought.

By the time I heard the door slam and took a defensive position, he was in the car and well into a hearty laugh. A look at the man finds me staring at three eyes. Two eyes on his face and the one at the end of the gun barrel. I pray that his heavy laughter doesn't cause his finger to accidentally pull the trigger. I have been meaning to start carrying a gun. But my line of work shouldn't put me in any harms way. Yet, here I am.

"You've got a lot to learn about being a private detective Mick. My name is, Frank, Frank Clark," says the man.

"Yeah?"

"If an old man like me can get the drop on you, you're in trouble."

"I guess so."

"Betty, inside said you're looking for information about Mary Jane Jenkins. The paper says that the police have her old man for killing her."

"That's right."

"So what are you looking for?"

"Someone else who might have wanted to kill her."

"Someone like me?"

"Maybe. What was the nature of your relationship with Mary?"

"What's the nature of my relationship? Do you know who I am?"

"Frank Clark by your introduction." The stocky man of about fifty-years-of-age reaches in his inside jacket pocket, pulling out a wallet and tossing it to me. It is heavy. Inside it, I learn why. Pinned to the wallet is a detective's badge for the Odelot Police Department. "Excuse me, Detective Frank Clark."

"Retired," corrects Clark. "Five years now, on disability."

"Okay. The question is still pending."

"Mary was a friend."

"That's it?"

"That's it. (*Sniff.*) She was the sweetest thing alive." Frank becomes choked up. "I met Mary and her kids at a Burger King a year or so ago. We hit it off from there. I'm tellin' you this cause it can't hurt any now."

"You're wearing a wedding ring. Did Mrs. Clark know about you and Mary's friendship?"

"Maybe. Let's say she didn't know it was Mary per se, but that there was someone."

"And she was okay with that?"

"Okay Mickey boy, let me tell you what was going on, to save you some time from chasing your tale."

"It's Mick, not Mickey."

"Okay, Mick. My disability came from me getting shot in the groan. I lost a testicle and psychologically, I lost part of my manhood. At least that's what the therapist says. Since the shooting, I haven't been much for getting it on in the sack with my wife. Sure she said she understood and has stuck by me through it all, but I know she has needs. I found out she has some *hot boy* that she meets up with every now and then. She doesn't know that I know."

"So Mary was your way of getting back at your wife?"

"No! Like I said, we met and we hit it off. You've seen her right?"

"Yeah."

"A beautiful girl. We began spending time together. We hung out here at the club. One night she had on this black dress that wrapped around her like cellophane. I mean she was looking good and I felt good to be with her. She danced with me and hugged up on me like I was everything in her life. She made me feel special in front of my friends.

"That night, we went to her place. After a few more drinks, she worked on me until my Johnson came to life and I actually got a nut off. I hadn't done that in four years of trying. That night I fell in love with that girl. I hadn't been able to repeat, but it wasn't for a lack of trying. But it didn't matter to Mary. She didn't look upon me any differently.

"Sometimes, we would just lay in her bed naked and talk. She was a good listener. I loved that about her as well."

"Did you know she was getting married?"

"Yeah."

"How did you feel about that?"

"I was happy for her. Somebody was finally going to do for her what I was doing for her undercover."

"It didn't bother you that you were losing a special friend?"

"Not at all. Especially, not enough to kill over. And why would I kill her and not the guy?"

"Because it was her choice to end the relationship with you and you felt cheated, used. Or maybe all wasn't as you've painted it. Maybe she threatened to tell your wife about your friendship in an attempt to blackmail you."

"Now you are being desperate. My wife wouldn't care one way or the other. Plus, Mary knew who her bread and butter was. Why would she want to burn her toast?"

It was as good a question as it was a good line. I would have to remember it when it came time for me to write my investigative memoirs. Clark was right. I was desperately trying to pin him as murderer or even a suspect. But he was a known man among the many in Mary's life.

"Do you know a guy by the name of Anthony James, he goes also by the name of Smoke?" I asked the retired detective.

"No. The only guy Mary ever mentioned was one of her kids' fathers, Double D.

"Double D?" I query.

"Mary said he likes girls with big breasts. His real name is Duane Davis. So take your pick for why the nickname. He's just moved to a halfway house and has been calling her. She sounded scared of him. He threatened her. If anyone other than the fiancé had anything to do with her death it was him. He actually told her that, 'if he couldn't have her nobody could.'"

"But you said he was in a halfway house."

"Right, on a work release program. He could get to her."

"Thanks Frank. I'm sorry about the accusations."

"Right. You've got a lot to learn about detective work."

"I'm an investigator. I'm investigating. Two more things Frank, what kind of car do you drive?"

"A Deuce and a Quarter. Why?"

"I'm looking for a driver of a black SUV."

"And the other thing?"

"How did you really feel about losing Mary to marriage?"

"Like I said, I was happy for her. Then again, who said I was losing her? Mary was used to a certain lifestyle. Some habits are hard to break."

~~~~~~~

That's just what I didn't need, another name to be added to my list of suspects. Duane Davis is the father of Mary's oldest child Sapphire. He's out of prison lockup at a minimum-security transition house on a work release program. He's had contact with and had made alleged death threats to the victim. That moves him up on the list of suspects. At least it moves him ahead of Anthony James, a.k.a. Smoke.

Less than five miles from Perry Rogers' home is the Odelot Transition House. It's a halfway house for minimal security prisoners on a work release program. Duane Davis is a resident at Odelot House. He has been in the work release program for a month. It's early, 6:15 a.m. early. I'm parked outside the facility watching the residents file out for work. The police file photo and description of the five foot two "Double D" is what I'm using to spot him. One out of the five guys heading for an unmarked white van matches the description.

"DUANE DAVIS." I yell as I step out my car. With a cool and calm, he turns in my direction. In reaction to my bellow the others jump to a halt,. They maintain a wall around the smallest member of their group. I approach them with a confident stride. My steps stop two feet from the largest of the crowd, a guy who looks to have taken full advantage of the free weights and the workout gym while being locked up. I look past him to Double D, who's caring a lunch bag and a book. My unyielding stare brings about a vocal response from him.

"You a bold man to be callin' out another man's name like you his daddy."

"Would that make you my son?"

"Oh, you got jokes. Just like most black fathers, you been absent so long you don't know what's the *dealio*. My name now is Elasha, whom God made. What chu want with me?"

"If you don't mind, I would like to talk to you about Mary Jane Jenkins. Alone." I eye each member of the crowd, remembering their faces.

"Excuse us fellahs." The men move on. "Yeah, so what'sup?"

"Did you know Mary is dead?"

"I heard. Police got her dude for it. So?"

"Mary's daughter is yours right? So you know about fathers being absent don't you?"

"Asked and answered."

"How did you feel about her getting married?"

"I was *straight* with it."

"Really, the word is you threatened her. 'If you couldn't have her nobody could,' I believe were your words. Is that right?"

"You seem to be well informed. I said it, but it was not because she was getting married to old dude. It was because I heard she was *kickin' it* with a *scrub*. Like I said, I was *straight* with her getting married to somebody who was going to take care of her and my kid."

"Who was this *scrub* guy?"

"Small time drug dealer who goes by the name of Smoke."

"This Smoke, do you know where I might be able to find him?"

"Why?"

"I just want to talk with him, like I'm talking with you."

"I thought they got the Mr. Rogers dude for killing Mary."

"Well, I'm not sure they have the right man."

"You came to me thinking I had something to do with her death?"

"Maybe."

"And I thought you were a smart man. I'm a man making atonement for my past life." Duane Davis, Double D, Elasha holds up the book he's carrying. The book's title, "From Niggahs to Gods."

"What are you reading in the book?"

"That as black men, we need to live *up* to our potential and not *down* to others expectations. Instead of getting understanding of the white man's rules, we need to be getting upstanding with ourselves." He continues to speak. "I loved Mary and I love my daughter. I would not hurt them."

"I don't mean to be disrespectful, but didn't you rape Mary, causing her to get pregnant with your daughter?"

"Yes. That was when I was a mis-educated Negro. I didn't know how to express my feelings for my black sistah. I didn't see my father show his love and affection to my mother. The only time I saw him express any emotion is when he got drunk and went upside my mother's head with his fists. That was my role model."

"That's a bunch of bullshit Duane." I say to him as he looks at me cross. "Excuse me, Elasha. You raped Mary Jane Jenkins, because you didn't accept no for an answer."

"You're wrong man. Mary and I had mad sex when we were *kickin' it.* Like I said, I didn't know how to tell Mary that I loved her before. I knew if I got her pregnant, she would be mine for as long as she had my baby. I forced the issue cause she didn't want any kids.

"Let me tell you about Mary man. She was *slammin'* okay. I mean the minute I saw her, I knew that I had to have her. She had them big *breastses* and a nice ass. I've seen her turn heads of old men and young boys. That was my only problem with her. The niggahs wouldn't leave her alone. We be walkin' down the street and muthafuckas would be yellin' shit at her, like I wasn't even there. So, that meant I couldn't leave her alone, without worrying about some niggah tryin' to get with her. That's why I got her ass pregnant."

Elasha smiles as he continues, "but the shit backfired. She started looking better after she got pregnant. Her *breastses* and ass got bigger. *Playa hatas* came from every where when I was sent up."

"I understand one of your own boys thought so. He raped her after you."

"*True that.* That's how I got to do a *nickel* more for assault while I was locked up."

"I don't follow. I was in the joint when punk ass Jackie raped Mary. When he came in . . . well, let's just say he's sorry."

"So why are you a changed man now Elasha?"

"Man, being locked up ain't no joke. Specially if you got somebody on the outside you bein' kept from. I loved Mary and she was my baby's mama. I didn't even get to see my child born. I did get to name her though, that was it. All I know about my little girl is what people done told me. I don't know nothin' first hand, you know what I'm sayin'. I ain't get to hold her or nothin'. Now, she seven years old and shit.

"Every day I'm in the joint, I'm thinkin' about her. That was the only thing that kept me from loosin' it up in there. That also made me realize I had to change my life around and make things right between me and Mary."

"Didn't you know she was seeing other men?"

"Yeah. But I don't blame her for that. She did what she had to do to take care of her and the kids. Once I got out, I was goin' to try to be there for her."

"What about Smoke, you knew they were *kickin' it* right?"

"Yeah. He ain't shit."

"I see. Do you know where can I find Smoke, he's in hiding?"

"I don't know, but if you say he had something to do with Mary's death I will find him."

"How are you going to do that from this place?" I nod to the building serving as Elasha's minimum-security home away from home.

"I got reach. I may be small in size, but I can get big on your ass."

I leave Elasha with my business card and I thank him for his time and any help he may be able to give me. Three suspects down and one to go; Frank Clark, Jack Daniel, and Duane "Elasha" Davis and now, Anthony James, a.k.a. Smoke. The previous three men all expressed their conditional love for Mary Jane Jenkins. Smoke is the last name on my list. He is my last chance witness to save Perry Rogers from conviction for a murder that he may not have committed.

I tracked down Jackie, the man who raped Mary the second time, causing her to be with her second child. That second child is Mary's son, Gerald. As Elasha said, Gerald's father is sorry for causing harm to

Mary. I found Jackie, him/her standing on a street corner dressed in women's clothing. His front teeth are missing, I noticed as he/she spoke to me. I had heard of the initiation dentistry of new prison inmates. The work is done to disallow the new sex toy from biting the *member* of his would be suitor. As soon as I mentioned the name Mary Jane Jenkins, fear mixed with anger flushed Jackie's face. He/she began to shout profanities in a falsetto voice and hurried off as fast as his/her high heel shoes would allow.

VIII. Kickin' It with and Carin' for Mary (Perry)

"We must become the change we seek in the world." ~~ *Gandhi*

Everything in our lives was going beautifully. Mary and I had been engaged for nine months. We were getting married in three months. What I had felt about Mary in the beginning was coming true every day we spent together. In her was the woman I knew she could be and was. Mary worked part-time in the cash verification department at the bank where I work. I spoke with someone in personnel to get Mary hired. Everyday Mary came home full of excitement and talking about being surrounded by all that money. Her self-esteem was high, when she considered the level of responsibility and trust she had been given.

When she wasn't working, she was at home planning our wedding. Mary being at home was important to Sapphire and Gerald. To them, Mary was now attentive and helpful. When they came home with their schoolwork, Mary enjoyed helping them. She, we became actively involved in their after school activities and programs. We were becoming the perfect family, and I loved it.

No, this didn't happen over night. Mary and I began couples counseling with the Reverend Lowdown at Holistic Salvation Church, where I am a member. Counseling was required if we intended to get married by him. The reverend suggested some separate sessions in the beginning to get to know us. From the private sessions with the reverend, he discovered that Mary suffered from *post-traumatic stress disorder*. She had been living with it since early childhood. The child and sexual abuse early on, opened the door for the physical abuse by men in Mary's adult life.

The reverend who has a degree in counseling, said the disorder attributed to Mary's emotional numbness. Mary rarely, vocally expressed herself affectionately. She would never initiate a hug of Sapphire or Gerald. It was the same when it came to me. We were the ones who would reach out for her. Though she never rejected our hugs and kisses, she didn't know how to do what she never received as a child . . . to love honestly.

Learning this changed our relationships. Some nights Mary cried herself to sleep. She talked more openly. I learned of all the painful details and incidents she had with the men in her past. After hearing Mary's painful ordeals, it was me who needed some personal time with a counselor. I chose the reverend. For the first time, I questioned whether I could deal with being with a woman with such a tainted past.

"I have to admit Reverend, at first, it was just a physical thing between us. I mean, that was how we started. I know sex before marriage is wrong and all. But I began really liking her for some odd reason." I confessed.

"You started liking *her* or what you two were *doing*?" responded the reverend.

"Both, but her mostly. Mary is the absolute mate. I don't mean just physically. When I come home from a difficult day at work, Mary is as attentive to me as she is the children. Bless her heart, though she probably doesn't understand fully the work problems that I would bring home, but she listens."

"So, now you have your cake, by having a woman that is attentive to you, and you can eat it too, so to speak, because she pleases you in the bedroom."

"It isn't just that. Reverend, I know I'm a good man. I know that I would be a good man to Mary and her children. I believe in my heart that if Mary could see that, she would be content with being a good woman to one man. I want to show her that not all men are like those who abused her."

"But are you doing this to make you feel good or to make her life better?"

"To make Mary's and her kids life better. I'm going to feel good regardless. Because I'm doing what's in my heart."

"That's good.   Yet, you have doubts about marrying Mary because of her past relationships with other men. You knew a little of her past before now?"

"I knew a little. I knew the fathers of her kids raped her. But either every man in her life took what he wanted from her or she gave it to them freely to prevent it from happening."

"Son, if you want a change in your relationship, there must be change on both sides. If you want Mary to change, then you must change. If you come to her as a lady and virtuous woman she will respond in that way. If you come to her as a harlot then a harlot she will be. You need to help her come to understand this; you are not what you think you are. You are what you think," offers the reverend.

"That's exactly the case when I think of Mary, as far as what I think she is. I had this dream Reverend. *I'm walking into a corner store. Sitting outside begging for money is Mary. She's much older, fifties, maybe sixties. Of course she still looks attractive, just trashy. She doesn't recognize me as I approach. Mary then asks if I have a dollar or some spare change. I give her a couple of dollars. She thanks me, then she asks if I want her phone number and she gives me this seductive knee-buckling smile.* I don't want that dream to come true."

Reverend Lowdown told me the biblical story of Hosea, who God commanded to marry a harlot. The harlot represented the people of Israel who forsook God to pursue their lovers of false gods, doctrines, ideologies and religions. Hosea's harlot, like the people of Israel, backslid time after time. God instructed Hosea to take back his harlot wife who ran off time after time, returning to her wile ways. Reverend said that through it all, God remained true and consistent with His promised blessings to the people of Israel, despite their backsliding. The reverend said that true love is unconditional and if it's true it could withstand anything. What I felt in my heart for Mary and her children was true love.

"Reverend, I doubt that true love can withstand anything."   I challenged.

"Anything my son," returned the man of God.

"There is something I haven't told you or Mary, that I think could destroy our relationship."

"Oh!"

"It was something that I have kept to myself, because . . . I don't know . . . I didn't know how to tell Mary. Something happened. I didn't really handle it, I sort of reacted to it, then ignored it. I'm pretty sure it was a one-time incident and I'm sure it won't happen again. My dilemma is whether I should let Mary know."

"A member of the church came to me once and told me of an affair she had. She said it was a one night stand, that she had no feelings for the man and that it wouldn't happen again. The woman asked me if she should tell her husband. - - - Some would say that what the husband doesn't know, wouldn't hurt him.

"But once you start harboring one lie and think you got away with it, then you might think that you can get away with others and thus the spiral to damnation begins. And I said, that you *think* you got away with it. Matthew, ten and twenty-six; *'Fear them not therefore; for there is nothing covered, that shall not be revealed; and hid, that shall not be known.'* Sooner or later all deeds will come to light and be revealed. You can determine when that will be." The reverend concluded.

The reverend was right, I needed to tell Mary about the incident with Sapphire. The question was when and how. Our lives and plans were coming along so nicely. At home, Mary took care of running the house if you will. Redecorating was the first thing on her agenda, having to make our furniture match. She took on paying all the household bills by learning online computer banking. It was impressive how well and quickly Mary mastered the software programs on my home computer.

Soon, she was virtually planning our entire wedding via the Internet. If you could have seen the enthusiasm on her face when she would talk about surfing the web and finding this web site or that web site. Seeing her enthusiasm was such that it spilled over into me. But I had my own excitement and enthusiasm. At work, I had received a pivotal promotion that set me above being financially comfortable. I was now well-to-do. Mary, her children nor I would want for anything. Everything was going along so well.

One day in particular, Mary gave me the confidence that all was well in our world. I came home as usual, but what was different about this day was Mary had a guest. It was the first time I had met a female friend of Mary's. Her name is Pebbles. Along with my introduction to

Pebbles, came the behavior that I almost thought was a performance. I mean I thought I was on some hidden video television show. After introducing me to Pebbles, Mary wrapped her arms around my neck, kissed me on the mouth, called me "Boo" and asked me how was my day. I didn't know what to say. So I said nothing. I simply hugged and kissed her in return. It didn't matter that Pebbles was watching our open display of affection.

IX.   Mary, Mary Quite Contrary (Mick)

Pebbles Lindsey works out of her home, doing hair for others. She has established a literal underground beauty shop, working out of her basement. She has one chair for the customer to sit in while she works on their head. There are two dining room table chairs for waiting patrons. I occupy one of those seats. Pebbles is cute, chubby after giving recent birth to triplets. The three baby boys play in a playpen in a corner of the makeshift salon. Pebbles is preparing her beautician workstation in anticipation of an early morning patron. She granted me the 7:00 a.m. opportunity to talk with her because she said it would be the only time she would be free. Business was good.

"So Pebbles, do you know where I can find a friend of Mary's named Smoke?" I asked the cherub woman.

"Smoke wasn't no friend of Mary's. They might of *kicked it,* that's about it." Pebbles responded without missing a beat of her preparation routine.

"Okay, do you know how I can find him?"

"Not really. I don't like mess, so I don't be around it."

"Tell me about Mary. I understand you were going to be her maid of honor."

"Yeah, well, that's in the past ain't it. Damn shame too."

"Yes it is. How long have you known Mary?"

"Me and Mary was girls back in the day. We grew up together. Best friends."

"Really. I was told she didn't have many close female friends."

Pebbles laughs to herself and walks out of the room. She returns carrying some supplies and begins stationing them around her working area. We sit for another five minutes before she offers a comment to my last statement.

"Like I said, me and Mary used to be girls back in the day. Women have a hard time bein' friends with one another. Some bullshit is always goin' to come between them. Most of the time, it's goin' to be over some dude.

"I ain't *playa hatin'* cause Mary was always a nice looking girl and thangs. Hell, the first time she came over to my house after school when we was in the seventh grade, she got my daddy *sprung*. Had my mama goin' off on him and shit, cause every time she would come over he would want to wrestle with her. Mary told me he would be rubbing on her breasts and ass."

"Did that come between you two?"

"Not really. That shit was between my daddy and my mama. Nah, Mary and me had problems when my so-called boyfriend at the time wanted to do a three-way with him, Mary and me. When I told him hell no, he asked Mary if he could just get with her."

"Did she get with him?"

"He said she did. Mary denied it, but I didn't believe her at the time. I knew Mary. She would use a *niggah* until he was all used up and then just move on to the next one. But hey, if they would go for it, then it ain't her fault. *Niggahs* would be in love with Mary. I seen some *hard brothas* cry over her. And I also heard bout niggahs almost gettin' killed cause of her too."

"Yet, you don't think Mary was to blame."

"No. No I don't. Mary was just bein' Mary you know. People couldn't 'cept that about her. They wanted to change her or keep her all to themselves. You could keep Mary if she wanted to be kept. You know what I'm sayin'?"

"I think so. Was she serious about getting married to Perry Rogers?"

"HELL YEAH! I was fucked up when she called me after we ain't spoke in years, talkin' 'bout she wanted me to be in her weddin'. I was like 'yeah right.' But *homegirl* was serious as a heart attack."

"Was it his money or what?"

"Nah, that's what I thought when I seen his *crib* and shit. I mean dude did have the *Benjamins*, but she told me she was in love. When we was younger, she only said that to me once and that was about Sapphire's daddy Duane. Perry was pretty cool. I mean he was different from the other dudes I knew Mary *kicked it* with.

"He took her and her kids into his crib, got her a job and he wanted to marry her. These other *niggahs* just wanted to lay up in her shit and *kick it*. You know what I'm sayin? This dude was the *fo' real Captain Save a Ho*."

"Somebody was with Mary the night she was killed. I have reason to believe it might have been Smoke. If Mary was ready to settle down, why would she call Smoke over."

"For some *bud* probably. Mary still liked gettin' high. She told me how she was goin' to miss it. She said she hadn't gotten high since she got the job at the bank. She had to take a piss test to get it, so she said she stopped smokin' for a while."

"So you think that's why she called Smoke over?"

"If she did, that's why. Cause she was through *kickin' it* with no good *niggahs*. She was ready to *chill*."

"Hmmph."

"So you think he had somethin' to do with whoever *kilt* her?"

"Yeah. I don't think Perry did it."

"I didn't think so either. I only known him for a little while, but dude was straight up in love with Mary and her kids, that Huxtable kind of love. It wasn't like her kids were no BeBe's. They were cool with him too. I sure hope Duane don't find out Smoke had anything to do with Mary, or his ass is goin' to be *smoked* for real. Duane don't play when it comes to Mary and his little girl."

"So I hear."

Pebbles was right. If Duane a.k.a. Elasha found Smoke before I did, he might kill him and I need Smoke alive to prove Perry's innocence. I left Pebbles' home beauty shop wondering what happened the night of Mary's murder. Had Mary called Smoke to bring her some marijuana? As a tip for making a home delivery, Smoke decided he deserved a sexual play in return. Mary, in her newfound love and life wouldn't give Smoke what he was used to getting, so he decided to take it. After raping her, Smoke kills Mary to cover his lesser crime. It doesn't make sense.

What does make more sense is Perry Rogers coming home finding Mary sexually assaulted. Once she explained who committed the act and why he was there in the first place, Perry goes into a fit of rage and kills Mary. Oh yeah, I'm forgetting my job is to prove Mrs. Rogers' son didn't kill Mary Jane Jenkins. Then Mrs. Rogers' son needs to start helping himself.

X.   Kickin' It and Killin' Mary (Perry)

We were supposed to have been working late that night. All week I was putting in overtime because of an internal audit at the bank. A computer server crashed and we were sitting around with nothing to do. Management sent us home early for a change. I was going to surprise Mary and the kids with pizza. I picked up my called-in order from Gino's Pizza and stopped at a corner store buying a bottle of Mary's favorite wine. I remember smiling to myself as I reflected on the act. It put me in mind of the early days of our relationship. Bringing home a couple bottles of wine would make for a long night of good sex.

Just as I pulled up to the house, I saw the black SUV driving away. I recognized it. It was the same SUV Mary went to that night at the club. It was the same SUV that was parked outside her apartment the night she wouldn't answer the door when I was on the outside knocking. I never knew who the driver was. I suspect also, that this is the same guy who moved himself in to Mary's apartment and physically abused her and sent her and the kids to my house in the early morning.

From this point on, I'm not sure of the details. I think I went into shock. I couldn't believe Mary was still playing around on me and in my own house. We were about to be married.

The next thing I remember was walking into the house and finding the kids watching television. I went straight up to the bedroom, where I found Mary, lying in bed. The room reeked of drugs, alcohol and sex. She looked at me with half opened eyes and smiled as though she had done no wrong. I think I remember yelling, but she just laughed.

Because I was still holding the pizza and wine, I took them to the kitchen. That's when I guess I picked up the knife. I went back up stairs to confront Mary again. Still, she laughed at me. She called me a fool. I told her to shut up and there was more yelling. After that, I just recall standing over her bloodied body. I swear I don't remember what happened or how. I don't remember stabbing her at all.

No one may believe this, but I loved Mary and her children.

XI. Mary Jane (Mick)

At 11:45 p.m., I receive a call on my business line. I had fallen asleep on my couch watching a late night preseason football game. Perry Rogers' confession should have put an end to my investigation. It didn't. It took several rings of the phone before I could discern the tones to be real and not in my dream.

"Yeah, Mick Hart," I got out.
"Be at 745 Belmont in fifteen minutes. Come through the back, in the alley," instructed a male voice.
"Who is this?"
"Be there in fifteen or Smoke will leave this earth without you hearin' what he has to say."
"No! Don't KILL HIM!" The phone went dead.

I rush to the door trying to remember the address. The drive to the neighborhood took just over twenty minutes. The fear that one or two too many traffic lights may have condemned two men to death. The alley is poorly lit, behind the abandoned house with the address given over the phone. A person steps out of the shadows and stops me. My headlights shine on a young man with a Snoop Dogg braid platted hairstyle. He takes one hand and signals me to cut my lights off. After complying, I stay in the car. I don't carry a gun. It's times like this when I always find myself contemplating why I don't.

The young man comes to my side of the car. "Follow me," he tells me. I recognize the voice to be the same as the one on the phone. We go into the garage behind the abandoned house. The garage is pitch black until a single low watt bulb lights the room from a utility extension cord. In the corner of the cluttered garage is a whimpering mass. I step toward the body, relieved that he's still alive yet afraid that he might not be for long. My escort halts my progress as he hands me a cellular phone.

"Hello." I speak into the phone.
"You have ten minutes Mr. Hart," Elasha informs me.
"I need him alive Elasha."
"That's sounds like a personal problem."
"No. That's your problem if you make it one. Murder carries more time than assault my brother."
"I ain't killed nobody. How could I, I'm locked up."
"Listen . . ."   "You have nine minutes." He concludes before disconnecting our call.

In the dimly lit area, I can barely make out the body mass lying in a corner. As I move in closer, the person draws in and spits out protests, along with coughing up blood. I can't make out the face for the bruises and swells. Inside, I know it is the elusive Smoke. His retreat to the corner is slow and painful, evident of his movement and grunts. I kneel down.

"Smoke. Anthony James?" I try to confirm.
"Yeah. Who is you?" answers and asks the beaten young man.
"My name Mick Hart. How bad are you hurt?"
"Why, you goin' to make it worst?"
"No. I had nothing to do with this."
"I told them I was sorry. Tell Double D, I didn't mean to kill her man."
"You killed Mary Jane Jenkins?"
"Yeah man. I tried to tell them boys, but they kept kickin' my ass."
"I have nothing to do with this Smoke. I just want to know what happened the night you killed Mary."
"You five-O?"
"No. I'm a private investigator. Why were you at the house?"
"Like I told them muthafuchas, Mary called me. She called me man! Ah shit" In his exertion to prove his point, Smoke pulls into

himself grasping at his rib cage. Undoubtedly he's suffering from cracked if not broken ribs. I look to the guy who showed me in.

"Call 911, this man is hurt bad." I yell to him. He looks at me and hunches his shoulders like, "oh well." He then walks away. I look back to Smoke, praying that he isn't hurt as badly as he looks. "Let's make this quick, so we can get you out of here and to a hospital."

"It ain't happenin' man. They ain't goin' to let me walk. Double D is crazy."

"Why did Mary call you?"

"She wanted some *bud*. She called me man I swear. I hadn't seen her *in a minute* since she *hooked up* with ol' dude right, the one she was 'bout to marry. When I see her code on my pager, I'm like *it's back on*?"

"So you bring the weed, then what?"

"Like I said . . . ah got damn . . . I'm hurtin' man."

"Tell me your story, I was only given ten minutes."

"What about me? What happens to me?"

"I don't know, but a innocent man is in jail because of what you did. I might be able to save your life if you give me something to work with. Saving your life might be worth it to me if I have an incentive. Jail might be your alternative, but it's better than dying." Smoke's head drops.

"SMOKE!"

"Yeah man . . . like I said, I hadn't seen her *in a minute*. I get my best *shit* to bring it with me. I'm thinkin' I can slide up in her, like routine, when we was *kickin' it*. When Mary opened the door to dude's crib; I'm like damn. I had not seen her look so good. Girl had dropped some pounds and was lookin' *phat*. She had me follow her up to the bedroom, I knew it was goin' to be on then. I was 'bout to *bounce* that ass."

"Where were the kids?"

"Shit, they was suppose to be watchin' TV."

"Suppose to be?"

"Yeah. That Sapphire came knockin' on the bedroom door. That girl never did like me. Mary told her to go back downstairs. She even had to go out and take her bad ass downstairs."

"So Sapphire knew you were there?"

"Yeah. Mary came back laughin' about how the girl was callin' me out my name and shit."

"Then what?"

"Turns out, Mary had us go upstairs so she could open the windows in the bedroom and smoke the *bud*. She didn't want her *niggah* or the kids to know she was smokin'. Mary had changed. After we did a *blunt*, I make my move on her right."

"You initiated the sex?"

"Yeah. We *rolled* before. She liked the way I *stuck* it to her and she liked it rough. But for some reason, she wasn't havin' it. Usually, after a couple of *joints*, Mary would spread them legs like butter. Girl had the killer pussy."

"So when she didn't give it up, you took it and then killed her?"

"Man, I don't know what happened. She ain't never told me no before. And I could tell she was serious. As good as she was lookin' I had to tap that *thang* again. But she started tellin' a *niggah* to get up off her and shit. I'm like, 'bitch, after all we been through,' I lost it. She pushed me off her and kicked me in my shit. Next thing I know, I hit her *ass* and I'm on her fo' real. While I'm doin' her, I got this chokehold on her neck to keep her still. Man, I swear I didn't mean to kill her. I was tryin' to be wit' her like we used to be."

"What did you do after you killed her?"

"I don't know, I just got off her and hauled ass outta there. I damn near tripped over her little girl when I opened the bedroom door."

"DAWG." My escort calls out to me.

"Yeah." I respond

"Phone." I go over to the garage door to receive the cellular phone.

"Yeah."

"Times up, my brother." Elasha informs me.

"Elasha, I need Smoke alive in order to clear Perry Rogers."

"I'm sure he told you what happened. You have your confession."

"It's no good without the confessor. It's considered hearsay. Elasha, how is killin' Smoke going to atone for Mary's death?"

"You've heard of justice. That's for the whites. For blacks, it's about *just us*. And this is between just us."

"Okay, so you prove that you're the big man. How are you going to feel being responsible for killing a man?"

"Too often, we lose sight of life's simple pleasures. When someone fucks over you it takes forty-two muscles in your face to frown."

"I've heard this one before, Elasha. And only four muscles to smile, right?"

"Wrong. It only takes four muscles to extend your arm and bitch-slap the mother fuckah upside the head."

"Okay your boys did their share of bitch-slapping and then some. What about the innocent man sitting in jail, who loved Mary and your daughter? Who's expectation are you living down to now, he whom God made?" There is a long pause.

"You're good my brother."

"I assumed you to no longer to be a niggah, Elasha."

"Give the phone to my boy. As-Salaamu Alaikum my brother."

"Wa Alaikumu Salaam."

Snoops Doggs' lookalike listens on the cell phone. "Aw-ight," is all that is said by him before disappearing into the night's shadows. I gather Smoke and drive him to Have Mercy Hospital's ER. Detective McIntosh is a grouch when awakened from a sound sleep at 12:30 in the morning. He agrees to come down to question and take a statement from Smoke. McIntosh has just as many questions for me, wanting to know why I didn't bring the police in on my case.

"I'll check this Smoke character's story. If his DNA matches the semen found on the Jenkins woman, that should be enough to charge him with possible sexual assault. We would also need to match his prints to those found on the victims throat."

"And get my client off. Your medical examiner said that the official cause of death was by Mary being choked to death."

"Your client still stabbed his fiancée. He's not going to walk away from this scot-free."

"But he didn't kill her."

"There is still the intent. I'm not sure what I can get him on, but I'll think of something."

"Why?

"Whether he killed her or not Mick, he wanted to. For me that's reason enough."

~~~~~~~

In the morning daylight, after I had gotten some sleep, I'm sitting in McIntosh's office. Every couple of minutes he's yawning. I'm beat as well. For me the case should be over, but I don't feel the closure. I discovered evidence that clears Perry Rogers of the murder of Mary Jane Jenkins. At the same time, I withhold Perry's false confession from my friend Mac and the police. If Mary was dead before Perry arrived, why would he take the wrap for her murder?

Perry's mother broke into tears when I delivered the news her son didn't kill Mary. That was the easy part. When I had to tell her that police still wanted to press some type of charge against her son, the joy disappeared.

"If he didn't kill Mary and they got the guy who did, why won't they let my boy go?" asked Mrs. Rogers.
"He did try to kill Mary. It's just that she was already dead. If she hadn't been, he would have killed her himself. I'm no lawyer Mrs. Rogers and I'm afraid your son is going to need one."
"They give him that public defense attorney, Dole Justice."
"I don't know anything about him. I'll talk with him for you."

After that phone conversation early this morning, I head for the Odelot Police Department's Homicide Division. Here I find myself looking across the desk of an old friend, who's pissed at me. He's studying a piece of paper, pretending to ignore me. Still, I act as if I did nothing wrong by not keeping him apprised of my discoveries. So I ask him a question.

"What do you know about public defender Dole Justice?"
"He's new, but good. Not good enough to get your client off."
"Of what charges?"
"I'm still working on that."
"What will be gained by charging this man, Mac?"

"Because letting him go doesn't add up? Why would this man want to take those kids mother away from them? Put her out of the house, but don't kill her?"

"You're taking this rather personally aren't you?"

"Yeah, I am. I'm thinking about those kids. Your boy Rogers is guilty of something. You don't intentionally stab someone nine times and expect to get away with it."

"I have to admit, I can't figure this one out myself. He doesn't catch them in bed together, but he comes in and stabs her, what, while she's sleeping?

"That's why you're not a detective Mick. We figure out the tough ones. I will have this figured out and air tight come trial day. When you want to play with the big boys let me know. In the meantime, you can work on this." Mac hands me a sheet of paper, which is a printout of an e-mail. On it is a math word problem.

"What is this, an entry test for being a detective on the OPD?"

"Funny. It's just a brainteaser. They help me focus."

Subject: Math Problem - Where the heck is the dollar?

Three guys in a hotel call room service and order two large pizzas. The delivery boy brings them up with a bill for exactly $30.00. Each guy gives him a $10.00 bill, and he leaves.

That's fact.

When he hands the $30.00 to the cashier, he is told a mistake was made. The bill was only $25.00, not $30.00. The cashier gives the delivery boy five $1.00 bills and tells him to take it back to the 3 guys who ordered the pizza.

That's fact.

On the way back to their room, the delivery boy has a thought . . . "these guys did not give him a tip. He figures that since there is no way to split $5.00 evenly three ways anyhow, he will keep two dollars for himself and give them back three dollars."

Okay! So far so good!

He knocks on the door and one fellow answers. He explains about the mix up in the bill, and hands the three dollars, then departs with his two-dollar tip in his pocket.

Now the fun begins!

Remember $30 - $25 = $5 Right? And $5 - $3 = $2 Right?
($3.00 to the three guys and $2.00 tip for the delivery boy.)

So what's the problem?
All is well, right?
Not quite. Answer this:

Each of the three guys originally gave $10.00 each.
They each got back $1.00 in change.
That means they paid $9.00 x 3 (guys) = $27.00.
The delivery boy kept $2.00 for a tip.
$27.00 plus $2.00 equals $29.00.
Where the heck is the other dollar?

Epilogue. Mary had a Little Lamb (Mick)

"Train up a child in the way he should go: and when he is old, he will not depart from it." Proverbs 22:6

I stuff Mac's e-mail in my pocket and leave his office with another problem on my mind to solve. Why does a man in love with a woman attempt to kill her? While searching for that answer, I might as well challenge myself with "why do fools fall in love"and "what's love got to do with it?" Here's my stab at the first.

Why do fools fall in love? Perry Rogers is nothing more than a brother in lust and love with Mary Jane Jenkins. This is why he got involved with the woman in the first place. A pretty face, voluptuous body a virtually free unbridled sex, this is what Perry lusted. That lust for Mary made him return to her the first time after the abortion of the alleged pregnancy by her former boss Jack Daniel. Sure, later he claims to have fallen in love with Mary and her children. So Perry goes back for round two.

This time, Perry sets up playing house with Mary at her place. He bonds with Mary's kids. A little too well, at least with one, Sapphire. She considers herself his little girlfriend. That notwithstanding does nothing in improving his relationship with Mary, which is evident, when she maintains to *kick it* with Smoke. Perry finds this out when he returns from a business trip, baring gifts for the kids. Perry is now a dejected and jilted lover.

Time heals all wounds they say, but what about the newly inflicted. Mary comes knocking at Perry's door with children in tow. She is battered and bruised by Smoke's hands. Perry opens the door to his home and his wounded heart and welcomes Mary, Sapphire, and Gerald. I suppose that's what love has to do with it. If it weren't for the love in Perry's heart for Mary and family, then he would not have made the gesture.

Love comes at a price. The highest price to pay for love is trust. Had Perry waived that price of trust, by keeping the sexual event between he and Sapphire a secret from Mary? Had Mary forfeited the high price of trust by her repeated acts of infidelity, those alleged or real? The answer is yes to both questions. There is one other person whose trust and love was broken.

~~~~~~~

It is early afternoon when I arrive at Teri Jenkins' home. The house is full of noisy kids running about. Gerald and Sapphire are amongst the rambunctious tikes. Teri has her infant on her hip. She tells me that Mary's children have been going to counseling to deal with what happened to their mother. "It haven't done no good. Mary raised her kids not to be spreading her business around. On account of the different men she would be *kickin' it* with. So I doubt they will talk to you." Teri informs me. I ask to speak with Mary's children, alone. We go into the kitchen and sit at the table.

"Hey kids, how's everything going?" This is about the safest question for me to start with.

"Alright." Sapphire answers for them both.

"My name is Mick. I'm a friend of Perry's. You know who Perry is don't you?"

"Yep," responds Sapphire with a gleeful expression, while Gerald nods his head on his sister's queue.

"He wanted me to give you some good news. Perry is coming home. The police got the person who hurt your mother. His name is Smoke. Do you know Smoke?" This time there is no reply from either child. Sapphire's demeanor does change slightly. A scowl infects her precious face. "Smoke told the police he came over to the house and went upstairs with your mom."

"She shouldn't of let him in!" Sapphire interrupts me, stabbing her small fist into the table.

"Who, Smoke?"

"Yes! He should not have been in Perry's house." She stabs her small fist into the table once more to punctuate her statement. "I hate her for doin' that." Gerald sits quietly by as tears begin to stream down Sapphire's face.

Perry Rogers walks into the kitchen with Detective McIntosh right behind him. Sapphire's eyes widen and begin to sparkle like jewels. She jumps out of her chair and runs to him, screaming his name. In one leap, she is in his arms. Instantly Perry's eyes begin to tear. After adjusting his hug of the little girl, Perry walks over to Gerald and puts his arm around him too. The little boy returns the hug. It is a touching scene. Though he won't admit it, I think Mac is emotionally moved. We give Perry some privacy, by moving into the other room.

"Why did you let him out?" I ask Mac.
"It's temporary." Mac threatens.
"Isn't it obvious that this man loves these kids and they love him. Right now, they need someone to help them get pass losing their mother."
"I'm not convinced Rogers is the man for the job. He's guilty of something. And I'm going to find out what." Mac makes his claim before leaving.

I return to the kitchen to find Perry with both children on his lap, hugging them tightly. It's an impressive show of affection. I'm convinced that this man genuinely cares for these children. Witnessing this show of love solves the problem that had been tormenting me.

"Perry, may I speak with you, alone?"
"No! We want to stay with you" Sapphire pleads.
"It's okay Sapphire. I'm not going anywhere. I will be just a minute. Now you and Gerald go and play with your cousins." Perry convinces Sapphire to leave. She does so with a pout. Gerald follows. With the kids beyond earshot, I let into Perry.
"It was Sapphire who stabbed her mother and you tried to cover." I make claim to Perry. He looks at me directly, but not with surprise.
"I don't know what you're talking about."

"I think you do. You lied to me. The truth is, you came home and found Sapphire standing next to Mary in the bedroom with a knife in her hand. She tells you what happened about Smoke. Sapphire was angry with her mother for letting another man into your house. Another man, who could upset her new happy home. Smoke was a man who would come between you and Mary and between you and Sapphire.

"Sapphire loves you Perry. She's your little girlfriend. You didn't know that Sapphire didn't kill her mother. To protect her, you took the knife and you stabbed Mary to make it seem like you did it. Your stab to her heart was probably symbolic yet it was your only stab. The other stab wounds were made by Sapphire."

"You are crazy. Smoke killed Mary."

"Yes he did. But he didn't stab her eight times."

"Nine."

"What?"

"She was stabbed nine times."

"How would you know that for sure, unless you counted? Smoke confessed to killing Mary, by choking her. There is no evidence that connects him to the stab wounds. We only have you for that."

"If you or the police thought that, then I would still be in jail."

"This is true . . . if the police knew what I know. Detective McIntosh believes you are guilty of something. He just doesn't know what. He will re-arrest you as soon as he finds a charge that will stick."

"He knows where to find me. If you don't mind, there are two kids who are waiting for me."

~~~~~~~

Outside of the courtroom, Mac and I wait for the trial to begin.

"How did you figure out that Perry was covering for the girl?" asks Detective McIntosh.

"The math was right, but the statements were wrong. Mary had been stabbed numerous times, but only one would have been fatal. Sapphire stabbed her eight times, but it was Perry who administered the ninth."

"But how did you know?"

"Like I said, the math was right, but the statements were wrong. Why would a man just learning that his woman was with another man, decide to kill her in her sleep. To Perry, that is how she would have appeared to him. No, he would have wanted to confront her. He loved her and her children and he had given her so many chances before.

"To an infatuated child, her mother was passed out and had just cheated on not only Perry, but their happy family. Sapphire became distraught and would do anything to keeping Perry in her life, even if that meant ridding herself of her main rival.

"Your little word problem helped me see that. The math in the problem is correct. The problem starts with the men paying thirty dollars for the pizza. It has you thinking one way as you try to solve it. In the end, a statement is wrong. The three men did not pay nine dollars each, which would make the x-factor twenty-seven. That statement of a mathematical fact throws you off as did Perry's stabbing of Mary threw you off."

Detective McIntosh was a man of his word. He brought formal charges against Rogers. After Mary Jane Jenkins' funeral, he filed charges against Perry for obstruction of justice. Brought up on formal charges, in court, Perry confirms my theory of how the events played out the night Mary was murdered with one addition. This was on recommendation of his lawyer Dole Justice. Before the judge, Perry Rogers recounts the night.

"I came home from a late night of working at the office. We were in the midst of an internal audit. All week long, I wouldn't get home before twelve. That night wouldn't have been any different, except the computers went down. We were told they wouldn't be up for hours, so we were sent home.

"When I came in the house, the television was on in the den, but no one was watching. I went upstairs, only to find Sapphire and Gerald standing next to their mother's body, in our bed. It was evident that she was dead. Both children had blood on them. Sapphire was holding the knife. They both had stabbed her. I thought they had killed her. So I made them get washed up and I threw their clothes in the washer.

"Sapphire told me about Smoke coming over and that he and Mary went upstairs together. I saw the empty bottle of brandy and the cigar tobacco in the ashtray. I knew what that meant. I was hurt. Clouded with anger and pain, I stabbed Mary to incriminate myself and to protect the children."

That was Perry Rogers' story and he stuck to it, as directed by his lawyer. Attorney Justice referred to it as an Affirmative Defense. The attorney contended that since Mary Jane Jenkins was already dead, the children committed no crime. "You can not kill someone twice. So then there is no victim as far as the children are concerned," he affirmed. Since there was no original crime committed by the children, the lawyer states, "then there was no obstruction of justice. Because there was no crime for the police to be involved in or involving my client." The pretrial judge agreed with the technicality of the law and dismissed the charges against Perry Rogers.

The judge did order continued *post traumatic stress disorder* counseling for the children. In the judge's words, "In light of what these children have been through, it is safe to say that Mary no longer has little lambs."

Perry Rogers filed for parental custody of Sapphire and Gerald Jenkins. Mary Jenkin's mother and sister spoke on behalf of Perry's good character. Pebbles Lindsey also appeared in court on Perry's behalf. The women testified how much Perry loved the kids. Also yours truly was summoned to testify. The truth from the way I saw it, Perry's actions were based on nothing but his love and protection for the children. When all was said and done, the custody court judge granted Perry Rogers custody of the children. When the judge gave his ruling, Perry Rogers let out a heavy sigh of relief and raised his hands to the heavens in a gesture of thanking God.

How will Perry Rogers fair in raising the children after the traumatic lost of their mother? Their lives will not be the same. I observed Perry reunite with the children in a group hug. The little boy was expressionless, while the girl was outwardly filled with glee. To most of the onlookers, the scene may be touching. For me, the daunting words of the judge may be too foreboding; "Mary *had* little lambs."

About the Author

Lawrence Christopher is a fiction author and writer of life stories and mysteries. Embracing the saying "the pen is mightier than the sword," to Lawrence the pen is less a sword and more of a feather to tickle the fancy of his readers. Lawrence Christopher began creative writing in grammar school, with writing poetry, before writing fiction.

Lawrence Christopher is a nationally published fiction writer. He was chosen as 'featured writer of the month' online at TimBookTu.com. TimBookTu is a Mobile, Alabama-based web site. It is from the online readership, which Lawrence Christopher credits for his accomplished status as a fiction writer.

Contact Lawrence Christopher at the email address, MFUnltd@aol.com or by writing him at:

MF Unlimited
Civic Center Station
P. O. Box 55346
Atlanta, GA 30308

Dog 'Em (The Short Story)

A Mick Hart Mystery

By Lawrence Christopher

It is an early-morning ride to the city morgue. I feel that the morgue is as good a place to begin my search for my latest missing person case. I want to start the case on a positive note by not finding the person as an unclaimed corpse. Amanda Monroe's aunt called me from Seattle, Washington to have me look into her disappearance.

"I'm an old woman, Mr. Hart, and I can't travel to Ohio."

"Yes ma'am."

"Amanda calls me every week and I ain't heard from her in two."

"Two weeks, ma'am?"

"Yes. The police told me they would look into it, but suggested that I give you a call; A Detective McIntosh."

"Yes mam. He's a good man. I'll do what I can."

I make a note in my electronic organizer to thank McIntosh right after I visit the morgue. I don't let Amanda's aunt know where I will begin my search. I tell her that I will go by Amanda's condo. I don't.

I tune in to the discussion on the morning radio show while driving to the morgue. The disc jockey has posed a question to his audience and is soliciting a response for a prize.

DJ - "The question once again, who was it who said 'can't we all just get along?' Go ahead caller."
Caller 1 - "It was Reverend Al Sharpton."
DJ - "Naw, man. Next."
Caller 2 – "Was it Mike Tyson? No, no O. J. Simpson?"
DJ – "You people are embarrassing. Now you know why there aren't many black people on Jeopardy. Help me out next caller? (Click) Hey don't hang up on me becuz I'm tellin' the truth. Next caller, I'm going to give you a hint. Though his national plea later became a national punch line in many animations, sitcoms and for talk show hosts across the country since, the person who made it was trying to bridge the racial divide after he suffered a brutal beating at the hands of police. Caller, make me proud."
Caller 3 – "Rodney King"
DJ – "Thank you, thank you, thank you. (Click) Hello? Did we lose the caller? Caller, you won an autograph copy of the book 'How to Train the Dog in Your Black Man' by our guess in the studio this morning, Chiquita Ali-Shakir."

I turn off the radio after setting my cellular phone in its cradle. I knew the answer before the DJ's last clue and being a black man, I have no intentions on claiming the prize, let alone reading a book with such a title. I wanted to put an end to the public humiliation of the black race.

Visiting the morgue has become too easy a routine for me. I used to get sick to the stomach every time I walk through the doors. After so many visits to start my search for someone's loved one, my stomach has learn to hold its own. The Medical Examiner and I are on a first name basis.

"Hey Mickey."

"Susan. How's life?"

"If I was keeping score, I'd say losing out to death."

"Any Jane Does?"

"One. If you had have come a minute earlier, I would have had two."

A glance into the stainless steel room reveals a scene of a grieving family viewing a body on a slab. I wonder what they feel more, the grief of losing a loved one or the relief of finding her. Before entering the room, I let them exit without looking at their faces. One woman is wearing a familiar scent that moves me emotionally. It is the same fragrance my mother wears every Sunday to church; Estee Lauder Youth Dew.

Once the group leaves the room, Susan directs me to a drawer. She pulls it open and uncovers the body. It is an African American woman who looks to be in her mid 20s. She fit the profile of Amanda Monroe, but it isn't her. Not according to the faxed picture I had received from her aunt. I turn to Susan's emotionless face and smile.

"It's not her." I inform her.

"That's good, right?" Susan asks.

"Good, right. That's why I start here first. How did she die?"

"She bled to death from injuries. Some joggers came across the body in the park, where it appears she was jogging too."

"Was she mugged?"

"Maybe. But the injuries came from the rape."

"Sad. What about the other woman whose family just left?"

"Same thing. Found in an alley near her apartment in the same condition."

"Whose got the case?"

"Your buddy Mac."

"Really. I have to stop by the precinct to see him anyway. Thanks Susan."

Not finding Amanda dead is just the way I want this case to start. A stop at the police precinct would normally be my next visit for answers, but in this instance the police gave me the case. Detective McIntosh and I attended high school together. We brought the state championship in football to our school. He was my center and I was the quarterback. We've remained friends and in contact since. I knock on the door to his office and enter. Mac sits at his desk playing solitaire on his computer.

"Mickey, come in man. What's shakin'?"

"Came by to thank you for the referral."

"No problem. Then you just came from the city morgue. One of the guys in Missing Person's knew we were friends and gave me a call."

"Why didn't your guy keep it?"

"We're short-handed with a bunch of loony cases. I have to pull guys from other departments."

"Susan told me about the rape victims."

"These crimes are making me feel like I'm handling the X-Files like on TV. A serial rapist who's boinking the women to death, if you know what I mean. I got drug addicts leaving their infected needles inside coin returns of pay phones and vending machines, which pokes people and infect them. Some sicko going to clubs and slapping stickers that have needles on them on people. And the needles are tainted with HIV. The sticker says, "welcome to our world." Man I ask you, what is this world coming to?"

"An end, yet you're sitting here playing solitaire."

"It helps me focus."

My phone is ringing as I approach my car. It is my assistant Verna.

"Mick Hart," I said.

"You're suppose to say, 'Take it to Hart.'"

"Verna, I knew it was you."

"Yeah right. The commercials are running and they are trying to convey the personal approach we give our clients in trying to find their missing loved ones. 'Take it to Hart Investigation Agency, and we will too.'"

"Okay Verna. Why are you calling?"

"I found Amanda Monroe."

"Where?"

"Have Mercy Hospital. I have a girlfriend who works there. She said that Amanda has been there for a couple of weeks. One other thing, she's in a coma."

"Thanks Verna."

This is still a good thing in my book. The case is solved, the person is found. That is the measure of my success. It is not my issue, in what state or condition the person is in. I still have to follow up to make sure it is Amanda Monroe before calling her aunt. I turn the radio on and the DJ and his morning crew are fielding calls on the topic of "ways to train the dog in your black man."

DJ – "As you know, we had author Chiquita Ali-Shakir in the studio this morning discussing her new book, 'How to Train the Dog in Your Black Man.' This has sparked quite a debate amongst our callers. Sonia, you've read the book right. What do you think?"

Sonia – "I think some of the advice Ali-Shakir gives is good in some cases. I believe the title and references used in the book take away the focus."

DJ – "You mean having the book written as if you are actually training a dog."

Sonia – "Exactly."

DJ – "How about some of the things she has written."

Sonia – "I thought the chapter on 'How to keep your Dog from Sniffing Other Dogs' was interesting. Here she says 'When you let your dog out of the house for the night, make sure to give him a treat, before he goes out to run the streets. Give him some {bleep} so he will be less likely to stiff around someone else's.'"

DJ – "Whoa!"

Sonia – "Now for practical purposes, I understand her idea. It's just the delivery."

DJ – "How about this. I want my female listening audience to call me with ways they have trained their men. Hello caller."

Male Caller – "Men wouldn't be dogs if women weren't bitches."

I turn the radio off, because I saw that coming. Black men aren't going to sit idly by and have their manhood subject to such ridicule by women along with everything else they have to fight against in this society. Now I understand the disc jockey's earlier reference to the Rodney King quote, in trying to ward off the discussion from turning ugly or verbally violent. "Can't we all just get along?" It's too late.

A stop at the front desk at the hospital and I am off to room 317. When I reach the room a nurse is in attendance. Amanda Monroe is a naturally attractive Nubian woman. She has short hair and is without makeup. I feel something as I look at her lying in the bed. The nurse looks at me wryly, before she speaks. She is a thick sister from the Islands. Her accent tells me it is either Trinidad or from the area.

"Can I help you?"

"I was wondering how she was doing."

"You her boyfriend?"

"No. I'm Mick Hart, a private detective. I was hired to find her."

"You are Verna's boss, no?"

"Yes. Are you her friend?"

"Yes. We talked this morning. Shame about the girl. So young and pretty."

"What happened? How did she get here?"

"It was a 911 call and our EMS brought her in. They said she would have died if she hadn't been found."

"Died from what?"

"I don't know if I should be telling you this."

"Listen, I have to call her elderly aunt with the news. She's bound to ask me questions. Or would you rather tell her yourself?"

"It's sort of crazy you know. Where I'm from you hear about it from time to time."

"What?"

"Bestiality. People having sex with animals."

"What?! What are you saying?"

"When they brought her in, her vagina was bleeding badly. She had scratches on her back and . . . dog semen in her."

I flash a look over to the young girl lying motionless in the bed. I can't imagine telling Amanda's aunt what has happen to her. Would I have to? I could tell her that I found her and leave it up to the hospital officials to tell her what happened. That wouldn't be "taking it to heart," I hear Verna's words in my head. I turn to the nurse with so many questions pursed on my lips, that they are trembling.

"Are you sure that is what happened?"

"Yes. I have seen some crazy things while working in the ER. Men come in with foreign objects stuck in their rectums, sometimes dead animal. Once a man came with a blanket wrapped around his waist asking to see the doctor. I asked him what was his problem and he insisted on seeing a doctor. I told him I had to know what the problem was.

"At the same time, I hear this low moaning sound coming from beneath the blanket. The man is keeping one hand under the blanket at all times. Eventually, we discover that he has his penis stuck in a cat. The cat was half-conscious and the man had his hands around its throat. The man's legs were all scratched and bleeding. It was the funniest thing we had ever seen. The doctors and nurses couldn't hold the laughing. The man didn't want to kill the cat he said, because he loved it."

"You're making this up."

"Honestly. What you men won't do sometimes for some goody."

"Goody? Apparently women go pretty far too."

I look at the nurse trying to contain my smile. The 'how to train the dog in your black man' topic of the radio show comes to mind. Then my thoughts jump to what McIntosh had told me. I did not know Amanda Monroe, but I refused to believe she was capable of bestiality, as the nurse called it. A young woman who keeps in contact with her old aunt wouldn't have such a perverse mind.

"Did anyone check for man's semen?"

"I don't know."

"Was there any sign that she had been raped?"

"The bruises and scratches we assumed came from the dog."

"Do me a favor. Find out if she had human semen in her as well. Here's my card. Call me or Verna with whatever you find."

I call Susan at the city morgue as soon as I get inside the car. She isn't in, so I leave a message for her to give me a call. Then I call McIntosh.

"Mac, it's Mick. What exactly did you mean by the 'rapist fucking his victims to death?'"

"What?"

"You said that this morning."

"The two victims we've found both bled to death from vaginal bleeding. He tore them up."

"Did you have Susan check the semen?"

"What do you know Mick?"

"I don't know."

"Why don't you come see me, then we can talk?"

"Maybe later. I have some stops to make. I'll come by later today or tomorrow."

"Mick, if you know something about the rapes, I need to know now."

"I just remembered seeing the family of one of the victims in the morgue this morning and, ahem, I took it to heart. That's all."

"Yeah right."

"I'll talk to you soon."

Mac's sudden interest in what I know tells me there is something to the rapes that is more than the run-of-the-mill. I drive to Amanda

Monroe's condominium and let myself in by picking the door lock. I feel guilty about the violation of her privacy in light of what I knew about her. If what I suspect is true, she had been violated enough.

The condo is well decorated. The rooms look barely lived in. There is a perfumed scent permeating the air, one I can get used to and would like to smell on my woman. I make my way to the bedroom, where I find the only disturbance in the house. The covers are half off the bed; paper is strewn across the room. There is blood on the floor and on the side of the bed. A trail of blood leads to the phone and the answering machine both on the nightstand.

There is definite evidence of a struggle. It doesn't appear that the room's condition came from a woman in the throes of having sex, even if it was with a dog. I pick up one of the papers off the floor. It is a page from the book, How to Train the Dog in Your Black Man. Why would someone take the time to tear pages out of a book and throw them all over a room? Answer: someone who was trying to make a point.

I find a bookmark amongst the scattered pages. It has a quote on it; *"Only those who will risk going too far can possibly find out how far one can go."* - - T. S. Eliot. Maybe I am wrong. How far has Amanda gone? The telephone rings, startling me. The answering machine picks up the call after three rings.

"Hey, this is Amanda. Sorry I missed your call. Leave me a message and I will be sure to get back with you. Bye."

"Mandy, it's Morissa. I didn't know if you heard that Tanisha is dead. I can't believe it. I will call you as soon as I learn more about the funeral arrangements. Call me, 555-9274."

I put the number in my palm organizer. I will call Morissa when I get to the office. I write the name Tanisha in my electronic organizer as well. I call Susan again from the car.

"Susan, did you get my message?"

"Yes, then I got a personal visit from Mac. He said not to talk to you."

"What? Why?"

"I don't know. I thought you guys were buddies."

"Me too. You didn't tell me everything about what happened to those women, did you?"

"I told you what you asked and needed to know."

"So what didn't I need to know?"

"Ask Mac."

"Come on Susan. This might be important."

"Sorry, Mickey."

"Can you tell me the name of the woman whose family identified her?"

"Mickeeey."

"Susaaaan."

"Her name was Tanisha Edwards."

"Thanks Susan."

When I make it to the office, there is a note on my desk to call Annice, the nurse from Have Mercy Hospital. Annice confirms my suspicion. There was human semen found in Amanda's vagina along with that of a dog's. If Susan would be as cooperative, I'm sure she would tell me the same thing about her Jane Doe and Tanisha Edwards. Amanda was suppose to die, she must have been left for dead. The question is, does the man who left her for dead know that she's alive.

If Amanda has been in the hospital for two weeks, and the person who did this knew, then an attempt would have already been made on her life. The best thing to do will be to keep it that way. I feel guilty once again. Keeping Mac in the dark might hurt our friendship. I owe him for referring Amanda's aunt to me in the first place. I will go see Mac right after I call Morissa.

"Morissa, my name is Mick Hart. I'm a friend of Amanda Monroe?"

"Yes."

"She wanted me to call about the funeral arrangements for Tanisha. She is too upset to call herself."

Morissa gave me the time and day of the funeral. I couldn't ask how the women knew one another. It would be something Amanda would have already told me. Now it is time to call Mac.

"Mac, I think my missing person and your murder cases are connected."

"How?"

"The girl in the morgue was Tanisha Edwards. She knew Amanda Monroe, my missing person."

"And how do you know that?"

"A message was left on Amanda's answering machine about Tanisha's funeral."

"You're making me sound like a recording. And how do you know that?"

"Other than I heard it, never mind."

"Have we not talked about obstruction of justice Mick?"

"I'm not obstructing anything. I called you with this information, didn't I?"

"Technically, yes."

"Now it's my turn to get information."

"This isn't about one good turn deserves another."

"Mac, you told Susan not to talk to me."

"I know. You handle your business. I handle police business."

"Your victims weren't just raped, they were violated afterwards."

"I thought you said Susan wouldn't talk to you?"

"She wouldn't. You just confirmed my suspicion. That's why you called this an X-File case. There's more to it than just a heinous rape."

"Listen Mick, I'm handling this."

"I'm just trying to help."

"You can help by staying out of it. Look for your missing person."

Mac disconnects the call. It is now time to call Amanda's aunt, a phone call I dread making. I can't tell her what I found out. So I tell her I have a lead on where Amanda might be. Eula Mae Monroe sounded so enthusiastic over the news, and thanked me profusely before we hung up.

Mac will have me followed if I know him at all. A police tail wouldn't be a bad idea if I did run into trouble. I will keep Amanda's whereabouts between Verna and me. Verna will keep tabs on Amanda's condition through her friend at Have Mercy Hospital. Three days later, there is no change in Amanda's condition.

The next thing on my itinerary is to attend a funeral. I sit in the balcony of the church watching the people file in. Funerals and weddings are both the same to me. I normally only attend them if I'm in them. The church fills very quickly. Tanisha must have been well liked. Where the grieving family is sitting is a group of attractive women. Morissa has to be one of them. The ceremony is long, with several selections from the choir, a number of speakers have kind words to say and children read poems. I stand outside before the church begins to empty. I ask around and have Morissa pointed out to me. She is a dark chocolate colored sister, who embodies the spirit of black beauty.

"Morissa, I'm Mick Hart. We spoke on the phone."

"You're Mandy's friend. Where is she?"

"She couldn't make it. I'm sorry about your loss."

"When was the last time you saw Tanisha?"

"It was at our book club meeting about three weeks ago. Mandy was there."

"How many are in your book club?"

"There's just five of us. Mandy, Veronica, Fana, myself and, well, Tanisha."

"Did you tell the others?"

"I called Mandy. Fana called Veronica. I haven't seen Veronica. There's Fana. Oh Shit!"

Morissa points in the direction of a woman who appears to be arguing with a man. Fana is beautiful. I know the word is sometimes over used, but it is right on point in this case. Even in a fit of anger Fana maintains her beauty.

"Who's the guy?"

"Her boyfriend. Ex-boyfriend, Eric."

"He doesn't look happy."

"You should have seen him a few weeks ago. He came to our last book discussion to confront Fana. It was pathetic. We all had to step to him before he would leave."

"Do you know why they broke up?"

"Yeah, the dawg tried to hit on Mandy. How are you going to hit on your girlfriend's friend? Mandy told Fana and she asked him about it. He didn't deny it. So Fana gave him the boot."

"Doesn't look like he's taking 'no' for an answer. Excuse me."

I walk toward the couple arguing in the parking lot. They had started drawing attention. I outweigh Eric by several pounds. So I am not worried about him stepping out of line with me.

"Excuse me. Is there a problem here?"

"Not unless you want to make it one. I don't think this is any of your concern." Answers Eric.

"Eric, this isn't the place to talk about this. I just lost a good friend. I don't have time for this right now," Fana said.

"You never have time for me anymore. It's always them before me."

"Eric, it just didn't work out between you and me."

"Eric, I think she wants you to leave her alone," I interrupt.

"I told you . . ."

Eric pushes me, catching me off guard. I grab him and we wrestle onto a car. The car's alarm sounds as we tumble to the ground. I am able to get Eric in a position of submission before the security guards come to break us up. We are separated and asked to leave the premises before the police are called. We are escorted to our cars by security. Morissa becomes a part of my escort.

"Are you all right?"

"Yeah."

"He's crazy. We told Fana he wasn't trainable."

"Trainable?"

"Yeah. The book we just read, 'How to Train the Dog in Your Black Man.' That was the book we last discussed."

"Did Eric know this?"

"I'm sure he did."

"Do you know Eric's last name?"

"Taylor. Why?"

"Just in case I want to file assault charges."

I ask Morissa if I could stop by sometime and talk. At first she is apprehensive until I assure her I am just a platonic friend of Amanda's. She knows that Amanda has not mentioned me before, so there could not be that much between us. We agree to meet later tonight around eight.

I call McIntosh to give him Eric Taylor's name. He isn't at the precinct. I have the desk sergeant transfer me to Missing Persons. The officer taking calls has a Veronica Morgan on his list. I told him, "check the city morgue. It's a great place to start." It is 6 o'clock; I have time to pay a visit on Amanda Monroe at the hospital. When I approach Amanda's room, I see Verna and the nurse standing outside.

"Mick, I tried calling you but your phone was off. Amanda has revived."

"Has she said anything?"

"No."

Amanda is barely moving any more than when she was in the coma. I step to the side of her bed.

"Hi Amanda. Your aunt asked me to find you." Tears begin leaking from her eyes. "Can you tell me who did this to you? You don't have to say anything. Just nod yes or no. Was it Eric Taylor?"

Amanda begins weeping at will, which gave me my answer. I kiss her on the forehead and tell her a half-truth, that she will be all right. The nurse replaces me at the bed. My first call is to Morissa. There is no answer. I look at my watch. It is close enough to 8 o'clock that she should there. I call McIntosh's precinct and tell the officer who took my call to have Mac paged. I tell Verna to stay with Amanda and find out as much as she can. I am heading for Morissa's.

I pull in front of Morissa's home. I see the lights are on inside. I call Morissa's number from the car phone. Still there is no answer. I decide to walk to the front door and ring the doorbell. A scream comes from inside the house. It takes me several attempts until I kick open the door. Another scream comes from upstairs.

"MORISSA!" I call out.

I run for the staircase. After taking the third step, I look up to find a huge Rottweiler showing me his teeth with a snarl announcing his presence. I freeze in my tracks. Walking up behind the canine is Eric Taylor, with one hand around Morissa's throat and the other holding a knife to her breast.

"Well if it isn't the hero of the day. You seem to be everywhere," he says.

"Eric, don't do this. Let Morissa go."

"This bitch ain't going anywhere. If it wasn't for her and her friends, I would still have Fana."

"Come on Eric. It wasn't their fault. You messed up."

"No. It was these bitches who messed up. All I wanted was to be with Fana."

"What about Mandy, Eric? Did you want to be with her too?"

"Not at first. When Fana and I had a fight, I wanted to show her that other women wanted me. I wanted to show her what she was about to lose. Mandy went and told Fana. I was going to tell Fana that she came on to me."

"Is that why you raped her and tried to kill her."

"What are talking about?"

"She's not dead Eric. The police know about the others too, Veronica and Tanisha. It was you who killed them." Morissa starts screaming.

"They tried to come between me and Fana. They kept telling her I was a dog, that I was no good. But I would have been good to Fana, if she would have let me. But they kept filling her head with that bullshit from that book."

"Let Morissa go, Eric."

"No. If I'm a dog then they are bitches. They deserve to be treated like bitches in heat, and get fucked."

"By you and Fido here?"

"Yeah and because you want to be a bitch hero, you're about to get fucked too. Kill!" he commanded the dog.

I see the scene in slow motion as the Rottweiler jumps from the top of the landing. All I can think to do is brace myself for the vicious attack. Suddenly, I hear a loud bang. It is a gunshot. The dog lands on me chomping at my forearm. He locks on to my arm, then collapses into dead weight. I pull my arm free of the dog's jaws. He is still breathing. McIntosh is standing with his revolver drawn and pointing at Eric. Eric releases Morissa, and she runs to me.

"How did you know I was here Mac?"

"I've been tailing you. I knew your sleuthing would lead me to who was responsible for the rapes and murders."

"You could have come in sooner."

"I didn't want to get in the way. You know, like when we played football together. I blocked, you got all the fame and glory."

"Nice block on the Rott."

Mac took Eric Taylor into custody. DNA testing was performed on him and the Rottweiler. There was a positive match to the semen found in the murder victims and Amanda Monroe. At the trial Eric was convicted for both murders and on all counts. Both animals were put to sleep. Amanda Monroe fully recovered with therapy. She moved to Seattle to live with her aunt. Mac and I met in the courthouse corridor after Eric's sentencing.

"Mickey, love for a woman will make a man do strange things. And your boy Eric Taylor couldn't handle the rejection. But to attack and kill innocent women," states Mac.

My correction to him, "You wouldn't understand Mac. It wasn't about the rejection so much. Black men are under attack from all sides of society. When it comes from our own women, it's worst of all. Then I recited a familiar quotation: *"Only those who will risk going too far can possibly find out how far one can go."* Just don't dog 'em.

The End